NOCTURNAL
APPARITIONS

BRUNO SCHULZ

NOCTURNAL APPARITIONS

Essential Stories

Translated from the Polish
by Stanley Bill

PUSHKIN PRESS

LONDON

Pushkin Press
Somerset House, Strand,
London WC2R 1LA

English translation © Stanley Bill 2022
This translation first published by Pushkin Press in 2022

'Undula' by Marceli Weron (Bruno Schulz), translated and introduced
by Stanley Bill, was first published on *Notes from Poland* on 11 July 2020
https://notesfrompoland.com/2020/07/11/
undula-a-newly-discovered-story-by-bruno-schulz/

1 3 5 7 9 8 6 4 2

ISBN 13: 978-1-78227-789-7

Frontispiece: © Polska Agencja Fotografów/Forum / Bridgeman Images

Typeset by Hewer Text UK Ltd, Edinburgh

Printed and bound by in Great Britain by TJ Books Limited,
Padstow, Cornwall on Munken Premium White 80gsm

www.pushkinpress.com

CONTENTS

FOREWORD

Stanley Bill

Bruno Schulz belongs to a lost world. He lived his creative life in the brief respite between the wars in the newly independent Poland of the 1920s and '30s. In this fragile moment, he produced a small body of literary works of the most concentrated imaginative power, before the world he inhabited was destroyed—and he along with it.

Born in 1892 in the small town of Drohobycz, then in the Austro-Hungarian Empire, Schulz and his native region found themselves in a south-eastern corner of the Polish state from its creation in 1918. Larger than today's Poland and located further to the east, the interwar state was dynamic and diverse. Ethnic Poles dominated, but minorities—Jews, Ukrainians, Belarusians, and others—constituted a third of the population. Plagued by internal conflicts, the new country was also a place of creative ferment, from modernizing construction projects to bold artistic experiments. It was here that Schulz pursued his creative career, publishing two collections of short stories and exhibiting his graphic works. And it was here that he made his living as a drawing teacher at the state secondary school in provincial Drohobycz.

Schulz's Drohobycz (today's Drohobych in western Ukraine) was dubbed the 'one and a half cities'—half Polish, half Jewish, half Ukrainian. His Jewish family seems to have given him a mostly secular upbringing in this mixed milieu. He knew German and probably understood Yiddish, but the main language of his life and creative work was Polish. As a schoolteacher, Schulz was a well-connected member of the local elite, though rising antisemitism created anxieties about his status from the mid-1930s. Many of his friends and acquaintances belonged to the Polish-speaking Jewish intelligentsia, though he also associated with Yiddish and Polish Catholic circles. His literary success brought him into close contact with some of the most celebrated figures of interwar Polish literature—among others, Zofia Nałkowska, Witold Gombrowicz, and Stanisław Ignacy Witkiewicz.

In 1939, the vibrant world of the Second Polish Republic was brought to an end by the dual invasion of Nazi Germany and the Soviet Union. By the war's end, the Jewish worlds of the region had been all but annihilated under the German occupation. In 1941, the Jews of Drohobycz were confined to a ghetto in appalling conditions, and then murdered in mass shootings and gas chambers. Schulz survived longer than many, having become an essential labourer to an Austrian SS officer who admired his artwork. The officer commissioned various works from Schulz, including fairy-tale frescoes for his child's bedroom. But this perverse protection could not last. On 19 November 1942, Schulz was shot dead on the street by another SS officer during an indiscriminate shooting spree.

In his lifetime, Schulz published only two volumes of short stories and a few other assorted stories and essays. His first book—*Cinnamon Shops* (*Sklepy cyna-monowe*, 1933)—was generally very well received by literati, though some right-wing reviewers attacked it, with an antisemitic subtext, for its supposed 'degeneracy'. His second volume—*Sanatorium Under the Sign of the Hourglass* (*Sanatorium pod klepsydrą*, 1937)—confirmed his reputation, and a year later he was awarded the Golden Laurel prize by the Polish Academy of Literature. Schulz was an avant-garde writer rather than a bestseller, but he was also very far from being an obscure or unrecognized talent, as he has sometimes been portrayed.

Schulz's literary output may be slim, but his writing stands out with the extraordinary distinctiveness and intensity of his style. In his descriptions of everyday events in the life of a family in a provincial town, all seen through the eyes of a child, Schulz created a private mythology of his own town, family, and childhood. His long sentences pile one wildly imaginative metaphor on top of another, creating a sense of excess, instability, and constant transformation, as ordinary objects undergo unexpected metamorphoses or reveal glimpses of mysterious inner lives. The plots of the stories are both easy and difficult to encapsulate: not much happens in a literal sense, while at the same time a cavalcade of fantastical events unfolds in the narrator's imagination or in the contortions of the language itself.

Schulz draws on various traditions of Jewish religion and folklore, mixing these elements and other mythological themes with the bathos of a shoddy, provincial modernity. The stories are rich in characters, painted with the vividness of a small child's perspective. Particularly memorable is the figure of the elderly father, who shares the name of Jakub with

Schulz's own father: an eccentric textile trader whose illness and madcap flights of fancy progressively drag him away from the world of his family in a series of disturbing metamorphoses. Schulz's tone is also unmistakable, combining emotive poeticization of the everyday world with an underlying irony that prevents the baroque excess of his metaphors from straying into kitsch. His style constantly teeters on this invisible border, which poses a fatal danger to would-be imitators and translators alike.

Schulz's career in English translation was slow to develop. In 1958, a translation of a single story— 'My Father Joins the Fire Brigade'—was published in an anthology of Polish literature. The translators were the extraordinary couple of W. Stanley Moss, a British secret services officer during the Second World War, and Zofia Tarnowska Moss, a Polish noblewoman and wartime head of the Polish Red Cross in Cairo.

In 1963, a complete translation of *Cinnamon Shops* was made by Celina Wieniewska, born in Warsaw as Celina Miliband—a Holocaust survivor and distant relation of later British Foreign Secretary David Miliband. In 1977, her translation reached a much wider audience when Philip Roth republished it in his 'Writers from the Other Europe' series with Penguin

Books. Wieniewska then translated Schulz's second book, as *Sanatorium Under the Sign of the Hourglass,* and the two collections were published together in a single volume in 1988.

Wieniewska's translations have been a stunning success, flowing and faithful to the poetic irony of Schulz's prose. It is thanks to her work that Schulz became known to English-language readers, gaining a veritable cult following among writers and artists. Wieniewska's Schulz influenced and inspired, among many others, Roth himself, John Updike, Cynthia Ozick, Jonathan Safran Foer, and filmmakers the Brothers Quay. Yet, in more recent times, some scholars, especially in Poland, have criticized Wieniewska's translations for their inaccuracy. Indeed, she seems to have adopted a deliberate strategy of simplification, occasionally even omitting whole phrases or sentences in the interest of comprehensibility. These complaints led to calls for a fresh English rendering of Schulz.

In 2018, Madeline G. Levine took up the challenge, publishing a new translation of Schulz's collected fiction with Northwestern University Press in the United States. She explicitly sought to redress the imprecision of Wieniewska's work, producing a version that hews as closely as possible to the idiosyncratic style and Polish syntax of the original. The result is a towering achievement and an invaluable broadening of the image of Schulz for the English-language reader.

My own rationale in accepting an invitation to embark on this new translation was first of all that great writers deserve multiple translations. Beyond this platitude, my ambition was to find a middle path between the 'domesticating' and 'foreignizing' approaches characterizing—in crude terms—the respective translations of Wieniewska and Levine. I have tried to capture Schulz's strangeness, never seeking to tame his complexity, while still erring on the side of the natural beats and structures of the English language—a recreation of Schulz's specificity in local conditions.

Where Schulz stretches the syntax or overloads a phrase with metaphors in Polish, I have also done so in English, but in a modified form shaped by the different tolerances and tendencies of the language. I have altered the syntax where necessary, while always striving to preserve the subtleties of meaning imparted by the original word order (Polish is more flexible than English in this regard). I have kept most of Schulz's long sentences and sometimes jarring repetitions, only restraining them when the resulting clumsiness or obscurity would be intolerable in English. In the end, such choices are based on subjective aesthetic judgements and an instinctive searching for equivalent (rather than identical) forms.

I have retained the Polish versions and spellings of names, including diacritical marks, as a simple way to immerse the reader in the unfamiliar sphere of another culture in a distant time and place. Most of the names should be relatively intuitive to pronounce, but a few are slightly trickier. The following glosses give approximate pronunciations for the latter:

Tłuja: *Twooya*
Maryśka: *Marishka*
Łucja: *Wootsya*
Jakub: *Yakoob* (Jacob)
Małgorzata: *Maogozhata*
Szloma: *Shloma*
Józef: *Yoozef* (Joseph)

The process of selecting 'essential stories' for this small volume was challenging. I have sought to include a diverse range of Schulz's works, while also giving the volume a coherent narrative arc of its own. The book includes close to half of Schulz's total literary output, featuring many of his best known stories from his two published collections. It concludes with a novelty: a recently discovered story, entitled 'Undula', probably Schulz's earliest work, first published under a pseudonym in 1922. Serving as a sort of epilogue to the volume, and accompanied by its own short introduction, this story gives a fascinating insight into the early development of Schulz's inimitable style and abiding themes.

My aim in this book has been to render a lively selection of Schulz's best fiction for the general reader in a style that is both accessible and true to his complex imagination. I hope these fresh combinations of Schulz's words in English might at least occasionally succeed in sparking what he called the 'short circuits of sense'—the electrifying new connections of word and image that restore language's visionary potential.

* * *

I thank Kirsten Chapman for her outstanding editorial work and for initiating the whole project, Elodie Olson-Coons for her fastidious copyediting, and the rest of the editorial team. It was a true joy to work on this volume with such engaged and professional support.

I thank Jennifer Croft and Rebecca Reich for their early advice and encouragement. I am also grateful to Jennifer, Clare Cavanagh, and Antonia Lloyd-Jones for teaching me so much about translation over the years, both in conversation and by example.

I dedicate this translation to Kinga, Andrzej, and Kajtek, who first introduced me to Schulz, and to all my Ukrainian friends in Drohobych and Truskavets—Schulz's native land, once again in the shadow of war.

AUGUST

I.

IN JULY, MY father went off to take the waters, leaving me with my mother and elder brother at the mercy of the white-hot, blinding days of summer. Dazzled by the light, we leafed through the great book of holidays, its pages glowing in the bright radiance and holding in their depths the languidly sweet pulp of golden pears.

Adela returned from the market on those luminous mornings like Pomona from the flames of the fiery day, pouring out from her basket the colourful bounty of the sun: glistening cherries bursting with juice under transparent skins; dark, mysterious morellos whose fragrance always surpassed their flavour; apricots whose golden pulp harboured the core of long afternoons. Alongside this pure poetry of fruit, she unloaded sides of meat, with their keyboards of ribs swollen with strength and nourishment, and seaweeds of vegetables like dead molluscs and jellyfish: the raw material for a dinner whose flavour was as yet unformed and barren; the vegetative, telluric ingredients of a meal whose aroma was wild and redolent of the fields.

Each day, the whole pageant of the summer passed through our dark, first-floor apartment on the market square: the silence of shimmering rings of air; squares of brightness dreaming their fervent dreams on the floor; the melody of a barrel organ, drawn out of the deepest golden vein of the day; two or three measures of a refrain played somewhere in the distance on a piano, over and over, swooning in the sunshine on white pavements, lost in the fire of the declining day. After her cleaning, Adela lowered the linen blinds and cast the room into shadow. The colours deepened by an octave and the room was filled with shade, as if plunged into the half-light of a deep-sea trench, still more dimly reflected in the green mirrors, while the heat of the day breathed against the blinds, which rippled gently with noontime dreams.

On Saturday afternoons, I went out with my mother for a walk. From the semi-darkness of the entrance hall, we stepped out into the sunny bath of the day. Passers-by waded through gold, their eyes squinting against the glare, as if sealed shut with honey, while curled upper lips exposed teeth and gums. Everyone wading through that golden day bore the very same grimace from the scorching heat, as if the sun had stamped one and the same mask on all its worshippers—the golden mask of a solar fraternity. Old men and youngsters, women and children, all greeted one another in passing on those streets with the same mask painted on their faces in thick, gold paint, grinning at one another with that Bacchic grimace: the barbaric mask of a pagan cult.

The market square was empty and yellow with the blazing heat, swept clean of dust by hot winds, like a biblical desert. Thorny acacias grew out of the desolation of the yellow square, their bright foliage seething above it in bouquets of exquisitely traced green filigrees, like the trees on an old Gobelins tapestry. It seemed the trees were simulating a gale, shaking their crowns theatrically so as to show off in grandiloquent excess the refinement of those leafy fans with their silver underbellies, like the pelts of elegant vixens. The old buildings, polished smooth by many days of wind, were coloured with the reflections of the vast atmosphere, with the echoes and reminiscences of diverse hues dispersed in the depths of the colourful weather. It seemed that whole generations of summer days had

been chipping away at the false glaze, like patient stuc-
coists scraping a mould of plaster off old façades,
exposing day by day with ever greater clarity the true
faces of the houses, the physiognomy of fate and life
that had shaped them from within. Now the windows
slept, blinded by the glare of the empty square; the
balconies exposed their emptiness to the sky; the open
entrance halls smelt of coolness and wine.

A little gang of tramps, sheltering from the fiery
broom of the heat in a corner of the square, had
besieged a little stretch of wall, attacking it over and
over with tosses of buttons and coins, as if the true
mystery of the wall, marked with the hieroglyphs of
cracks and scratches, could be read like a horoscope
from those metal discs. The square was empty. One
half-expected to see the Good Samaritan's donkey
being led in by the bridle under the shade of the swaying acacias to a vaulted entrance hall lined with wine-
maker's barrels, and that two servants would tenderly
lift the sick man down from his feverish saddle and
carry him carefully up the cool steps to a first floor
fragrant with the Sabbath.

And so my mother and I strolled down the two
sunny sides of the market square, dragging our broken
shadows over all the buildings, as if across a keyboard.
The little squares of the cobblestones passed slowly

under our soft, flat steps: some of them pale pink like human skin; others gold and blue; all of them flat, warm, and velvety in the sun, like sunny faces trampled by many feet into anonymity, into blissful nothingness.

At last, on the corner of Stryj Street, we entered the shade of the pharmacy. In its wide window, a great pitcher of raspberry juice symbolized the coolness of balms that could soothe every ailment. Only a few buildings further on, the street could no longer keep up its urban decorum—like a peasant returning to his native village, steadily stripping off the trappings of metropolitan elegance along the way to turn back into a ragged bumpkin.

The little suburban houses were drowning, plunged right up to their windows in the luxuriant, tangled growth of their gardens. Forgotten by the vast day, all manner of plants, flowers, and weeds proliferated luxuriantly, glad of this respite, through which they could slumber on the margins of time, on the frontiers of the infinite day. A gigantic sunflower, hoisted up on a thick stalk and apparently afflicted with elephantiasis, waited in yellow mourning through the last, sad days of its life, bowed beneath the excess of its monstrous corpulence. Naïve suburban bluebells and calicos stood helplessly by in their starched pink and white shirts, vulgar little flowers uncomprehending of the sunflower's tragedy.

2.

A tangled thicket of grasses, weeds, bushes, and thistles ran riot in the fire of the afternoon. The garden's afternoon nap buzzed with a swarm of flies. Golden stubble roared like red locusts in the sun; crickets screamed in the heavy rain of fire; seed pods exploded quietly like grasshoppers.

Close to the fence, a sheepskin of grass rose in a hunchback mound, as if the garden had turned on its side in its sleep, its broad peasant shoulders inhaling the silence of the earth. Upon those garden shoulders, the slovenly, womanish fertility of August was magnified in a quiet hollow of giant burdocks, which ran wild in furry sheets of leaves and exuberant tongues of fleshy green. The bulging effigies of the burdocks spread out like old crones seated on the ground, half devoured by their own frenzied skirts. Free of charge, the garden gave away its cheapest groats of elder, thick kasha of plantain reeking of soap, wild aqua vitae of mint, and all manner of the worst trash of August. But on the other side of the fence—beyond this summer nursery, where the idiocy of the crazed weeds proliferated—was a rubbish heap wildly overgrown with thistles. No one knew it was there that the August of that summer performed its great pagan orgy. On the rubbish heap, leaning against the fence and overgrown with elder, was the bed of the imbecile girl, Tłuja. For that is what we all called her. The bed stood on a pile of refuse, old pots, scraps, slippers, rubble and debris, painted green and propped up on two old bricks in place of its missing legs.

The air over the rubble had run wild in the heat, intersected by lightning flights of glistening horseflies driven mad by the sun, crackling as if with invisible rattles, which whipped everything into a frenzy.

Tłuja sits crouched in yellow bedding and rags. Her large head bristles with the rough bale of her black hair. Her face is scrunched up like the bellows of a concertina. Every so often, a grimacing sob crumples it up into a thousand intersecting folds, before astonishment stretches it back out again, smoothing out the folds and exposing the slits of little eyes and moist gums with yellow teeth below a snoutish, fleshy lip. Hours pass by, filled with heat and boredom, while Tłuja mutters to herself under her breath or dozes off, whimpering and grunting. Flies settle all over her motionless form in a thick swarm. Then suddenly the whole heap of dirty rags, strips, and sheets begins to move, as if animated by a scuttling nest of rats breeding inside it. The flies start with alarm and rise in a great whining swarm, filled with furious buzzing, flashing, and shimmering. And as the rags fall to the ground and scatter over the trash heap like frightened rats, the heart of the mass begins to unwrap itself, digging itself out, stripping away the husk to reveal the core of the pile. The half-naked, tanned idiot girl slowly drags herself up, like a pagan idol rising onto short, childlike legs; a bestial shriek erupts from a neck bloated with a rush of anger, from a reddened face darkening with rage, as arabesques of swollen veins bloom like barbaric paintings—a hoarse shriek ripped out of the bronchi and pipes of a half-animal, half-divine breast. The sunburnt thistles scream; the burdocks puff themselves up and flaunt their shameless flesh; weeds slobber with glistening venom; and the idiot girl, hoarse with the screaming and in wild convulsions, thrusts her fleshy loins with frenzied violence against the trunk of an elder tree, which creaks quietly under the assault of her wanton lust, exhorted by that whole impoverished choir into a degenerate, pagan fertility.

Thuja's mother hires herself out to housewives to scrub their floors. She is a small woman, yellow as saffron, leaving her saffron traces on the floors, fir tables, seats, and sleeping benches she cleans in shabby rooms. Adela once took me to the house of that old Maryśka. It was early in the morning when we entered her small room, whitewashed a shade of blue, with its beaten earth floor bathed in bright yellow sunshine amidst a morning silence punctuated only by the dreadful rattle of the peasant clock on the wall. In a chest on some straw lay the imbecile Maryśka, white as a sheet and quiet as a glove from which a hand has just slipped out. As if to take advantage of her slumber, the silence chattered away to itself—a yellow, garish, malicious silence conducting loud monologues and disputations with itself, vulgarly spinning out its maniacal soliloquy. Maryśka's time, a time imprisoned in her soul, emerged from within her, terrifyingly real; it rampaged about the room in a pounding, diabolical fury, rising out of the clock-mill in the bright silence of the morning like cheap flour, loose flour, the moronic flour of the insane.

3.

In one of those little houses, behind a brownish fence and drowning in the luxuriant greenery of the garden, lived Aunt Agata. When we paid her a visit, we came in past the coloured glass balls on little poles in her garden: pink, green, and violet globes in which bright, luminous worlds had been magically sealed like idyllic, happy visions enclosed within the incomparable perfection of soap bubbles.

In the semi-darkness of the entrance hall, with its faded oleographs devoured by mould and blind with age, we smelt the familiar odour. That faithful old smell contained the whole life of these people in a strangely simple synthesis, an alembic of their race, the species of their blood, and the secret of their fate, imperceptibly distilled in the everyday passing of their own separate time. A wise old door whose dark sighs had let them in and out—a silent witness to the comings and goings of mother, daughters, and sons—opened noiselessly like the frame of a wardrobe, and we entered their life. They sat as if in the shadow of their own fate, defenceless, betraying their secret to us from their first awkward gestures. Were we not, after all, bound to them by both blood and fate?

The room was dark and velvety in gold-patterned, navy blue upholstery, and yet the echo of the fiery day still flickered even here in the brass of the picture frames, door handles, and golden skirting boards, filtered through the dense greenery of the garden.

Aunt Agata loomed against the wall, large and luxuriant, her pale, plump flesh dotted red with a rust of
freckles. We sat down with them, as if on the very
brink of their fate, a little ashamed of the defenceless-
ness with which they told us everything without
compunction, sipping water with rose syrup, a most
peculiar drink in which I found the deepest essence of
that scorching Saturday.

My aunt lamented. This was the basic tone of her
conversations, the voice of that white and fertile flesh
bursting beyond the borders of her person, only
loosely kept within the bounds of an individual form,
and even in this form already swollen and ready to
disintegrate, branch out, and disperse into the family.
It was a fertility of an almost self-generating kind, a
pathologically luxuriant and unbridled femininity.

It seemed that even the faintest whiff of masculinity—the scent of tobacco smoke or a bachelor's joke—
could stimulate that inflamed femininity into wanton
parthenogenesis. Indeed, all her complaints about her
husband or the servants and her worries about the
children were but the fussing and sulking of an unful-
filled fertility, a continuation of the brusque, angry,
tearful coquetry that she inflicted in vain on her
husband. Uncle Marek—small, hunched over, his face
drained of his sex—sat there in his own grey

bankruptcy, resigned to his fate in the shadow of the boundless contempt in which he seemed to languish. His grey eyes flickered with the distant fire of the garden, smeared across the window. Sometimes he tried with a feeble motion to express some reservation, to resist, but the wave of self-sufficient femininity hurled aside his meaningless gesture, surging around him and spilling over the last gasp of his masculinity in a wide stream.

There was something tragic in that sloppy and immoderate fertility: the misery of a creature struggling on the border of nothingness and death; the strange heroism of a femininity triumphant in its fecundity over the deformity of nature and the insufficiency of man. Yet her progeny revealed the cause of that maternal panic, that frenzy of birthing that had exhausted itself in abortive foetuses and an ephemeral generation of phantoms without blood or faces.

Łucja entered, a girl of medium height, with head overgrown and too mature for her childish, chubby frame of white, delicate flesh. She offered me her doll-like hand, which seemed to be just budding, and at once her whole face came into bloom, like a peony flushing a shade of deep pink. Mortified at her blushes, which shamelessly revealed the secrets of menstruation, she closed her eyes and blushed still more violently at the touch of even the most innocuous question, each of which seemed to contain hidden allusions to her oversensitive maidenhood.

Emil, the oldest of my cousins, with his bright blond moustache and a face that life seemed to have wiped clean of any expression, walked to and fro about the room, his hands buried in the pockets of his pleated trousers.

His elegant, expensive attire bore the stamp of the exotic countries from which he had recently returned. His face, withered and clouded, seemed day by day to be forgetting itself, turning into an empty white wall covered with a pale network of veins, in which the dwindling memories of a tumultuous and wasted life intertwined like the lines on a faded map. He was good at card tricks, smoked long, elegant pipes, and exuded the peculiar scent of faraway countries. With his eyes wandering over distant memories, he told strange anecdotes, which always broke off abruptly, disinte-grating and dissipating into nothingness. I followed him admiringly with my eyes, hoping that he might turn his attention to me and save me from the torments of boredom. And indeed it seemed that he had winked at me as he went into the next room. I headed after him. He was sitting slumped down in a low couch, his knees crossed almost as high as his head, which was bald as a billiard ball. It seemed almost as if his clothes were lying there by themselves, pleated, crumpled, flung across the chair. His face was the mere breath of a face—a streak that some unknown passer-by had left behind in the air. He held a wallet in pale, blue-enamelled hands, inspecting something inside it.

From the mist of his face, the bulging white membrane of a pale eye opened with an effort, teasing me with a playful wink. I felt an irresistible liking for him. He took me between his knees and shuffled some photographs before my eyes with his dexterous hands, showing me images of naked women and boys in strange positions. I leant against him and peered at those delicate human bodies with distant, unseeing eyes, as the fluid of a vague agitation that had suddenly clouded the air reached me, running through me in a shiver of anxiety, a wave of sudden understanding. In the meantime, the haze of a smile that had appeared under his soft, beautiful moustache, the germ of desire that had stretched across his temple in a pulsing vein, the tension holding his features together for a moment, fell back into nothingness, and his face departed into absence, forgot itself, and disintegrated.

VISITATION

IN THOSE DAYS our town was already falling ever
further into the chronic greyness of dusk, its edges
overgrown with a lichen of shadow, a fluffy mould, a
moss the colour of iron.

Scarcely disgorged from the brown smoke and mist
of the morning, the day slid straight into an amber-
coloured afternoon, paused for a moment, transparent and golden as dark ale, and then descended into
the fragmented, fantastical vaults of the sprawling,
colourful night.

We lived on the market square in one of those dark
houses with blank, blind façades so difficult to distinguish from one another.

This resemblance was the cause of constant misunderstandings. Having entered the wrong entrance hall
or climbed the wrong stairs, one found oneself in a

labyrinth of unknown apartments, porches, and unexpected doors into unfamiliar courtyards, forgetting the original purpose of one's visit and only recalling the family home days later, after many strange and convoluted adventures, amidst pangs of conscience at some grey hour of dawn.

Filled with enormous wardrobes, deep sofas, pale mirrors, and trashy artificial palms, our apartment was falling ever further into a state of neglect, thanks to the negligence of my mother, who sat in the shop all day, and the indolence of the slender-limbed Adela, who spent her days unsupervised in front of mirrors at an extended toilette, leaving the traces everywhere in the form of stray hairs, combs, discarded slippers, and corsets.

The apartment had an indefinite number of rooms, as nobody could remember how many of them had been rented out to lodgers. Many times we opened one of these forgotten chambers by chance only to find it empty; the lodger had long since moved out, and we made unexpected discoveries in drawers that had lain untouched for months.

The shop assistants lived in the downstairs rooms, and their moans from the nightmares haunting their sleep often woke us at night. In winter, it was still pitch-black outside when Father went down to those cold, dark rooms, his candle scattering flocks of shadows, which fled headlong across the walls and floor. He roused the snoring shop assistants from a slumber as heavy as stone.

In the light of the single candle left behind by Father, they rolled lazily out of dirty covers, sat up on the edge of their beds, stuck out their ugly bare feet, and with socks in hands gave themselves over for another moment to the pleasure of yawning—a yawning prolonged almost to the point of lechery, a painful spasm of the palate, like a violent retching.

Huge cockroaches crouched motionless in the corners of the room, made enormous by their own shadows, which the flickering candle flung onto them and from which they could not be detached, even when those flat, headless bodies suddenly scuttled off in an uncanny, spidery motion.

At that time, my father's health was already beginning to fail. In the first weeks of that early winter, he spent whole days in bed, surrounded by flasks, pills, and accounts ledgers brought to him from the shop counter. The bitter odour of illness settled to the bottom of the room, as the wallpaper thickened with an ever darker tangle of arabesques.

In the evenings, when Mother came back from the shop, Father was excitable and prone to quarrelling.

He would accuse her of sloppiness in the accounts, flushing bright red and working himself up into a frenzy. Once I woke in the middle of the night to find him running to and fro over the leather sofa, barefoot in just his nightshirt, declaiming his irritation before my hapless mother.

On other days, he was calm and focused, immersing himself in his ledgers, lost in the labyrinths of intricate calculations.

I can still see him there in the light of a smoking lamp, perched among the pillows against the great carved head of his bed, with the enormous shadow of his head on the wall above him, nodding in silent meditation.

At certain moments, he would lift his head out of the accounts, as if to draw breath, opening his mouth, clucking his dry, bitter tongue with disgust, peering about helplessly as if searching for something.

Sometimes he would quietly steal out of bed into the corner of the room, where a trusty instrument hung on the wall. It was a kind of water clock or great glass vial, marked in ounces and filled with dark fluid. My father would attach himself to the instrument with a long rubber tube, like a twisted, painful umbilical cord, and thus connected to this pathetic device he would freeze with concentration, his eyes darkening and an expression of suffering or a sort of degenerate pleasure creeping over his pale face.

Then, once again, came days of quiet, attentive labour intertwined with lonely monologues. As he sat there in the light of the table lamp, among the pillows of his enormous bed, the room expanded over him in the shadow of a lampshade that seemed to join it to the vast element of the urban night outside. He sensed without looking that the space was growing above him in a pulsating thicket of wallpaper filled with whispers, hisses, and lisping sounds. He heard without seeing those plots of the night, filled with conspiratorial winks among the flowers of auricles that listened and dark mouths that laughed.

He pretended to be even more immersed in his work, counting and adding things up, afraid to reveal the fury rising up inside him, fighting the temptation to fling himself blindly forward with a sudden cry to seize handfuls of those frizzy arabesques, those bunches of eyes and ears that bred the night out of themselves, growing and multiplying, absorbing ever new shoots and branches from the maternal navel of darkness. He calmed down only with the ebbing of the night, as the wallpaper withered and curled up, losing its leaves and flowers, which thinned out autumnally to let in the distant dawn.

Then, amidst the chatter of the wallpaper birds in the yellow winter dawn, he would doze off for a few hours of thick, black sleep.

For days or weeks at a time, while seemingly plunged deep in the complex currents of accounting, his mind was secretly venturing into the labyrinths of his own intestines. He held his breath and listened. And when his eyes returned from those depths, whitened and cloudy, they calmed him with a smile. Still he refused to believe the claims and proposals that pressed themselves upon him, rejecting them as absurd.

In the daylight, they were like reasoned arguments and propositions, monotonous discussions conducted in a half-whisper, filled with humorous interludes and light-hearted banter. But at night they raised their voices with passionate fervour. The call returned more sonorously and distinctly, and we heard him conversing with God, pleading as if recoiling from something that was persistently being demanded or required of him.

Until, one night, the voice swelled ominously and irresistibly, demanding that he bear witness to it with his lips and his insides. We heard the spirit enter him as he rose from his bed, growing tall with prophetic anger, choking on strident words as he spat them out like a mitrailleuse. We heard the clamour of battle and the wailing of my father, the wailing of a tyrant with a broken hip, still hurling out abuse.

I have never seen the prophets of the Old Testament, but at the sight of this man, overwhelmed with divine anger, standing with legs wide apart on an enormous porcelain urinal, amidst a gale of waving arms, a cloud of desperate contortions, above which his voice rose ever higher, alien and hard, I understood the divine anger of the holy men.

It was a dialogue as menacing as the language of lightning. The contortions of his hands tore the sky to shreds, and the face of Jehovah appeared in the cracks, swollen with anger and spitting out curses. Without even looking, I saw him: a menacing Demiurge reclining on darkness as if upon Mount Sinai, resting a heavy hand on the curtain rail as he pressed his enormous face to the upper panes of the window, his fleshy nose squashed monstrously against the glass.

I could hear his voice in the pauses of my father's prophetic tirade; I could hear the almighty snarl of his swollen lips as they rattled the windowpanes, mingling with the explosions of my father's entreaties, laments, and threats.

Sometimes the voices died down to a quiet murmur, like the chattering of the wind in the chimney at night, before erupting once again in a raucous uproar, a tempest of confused sobbing and curses. Suddenly the window opened with a dark yawn and a sheet of darkness wafted through the room.

In a flash of lightning, I saw my father in fluttering bedclothes as he let out a terrifying imprecation and poured out the contents of the chamber pot with a mighty rush into the night, which roared like a shell.

2.

My father was slowly disappearing, withering away before our eyes.

Hunkered down between large pillows, the clumps of his grey hair bristling wildly, he muttered to himself under his breath, entirely absorbed in his own complex internal affairs. It seemed that his personality had disintegrated into multiple divergent and quarrelling selves. As he argued loudly with himself—passionately negotiating, entreating, and appealing—he almost seemed to be presiding over a whole assembly of petitioners, whom he was striving to reconcile with great ardour and gusto. But on each occasion those raucous gatherings, filled with fiery tempers, would disintegrate amidst curses, insults, and profanities.

Then came a period of muted quietness, inner peace, a blissful equanimity of the soul.

Once again, the great folios were spread out on the bed, table, and floor, and a kind of Benedictine calm of quiet labour hung in the light of the lamp over the white bedsheet and the bowed grey head of my father.

But when Mother finally came back from the shop late in the evening, Father would revive, calling her to him and proudly showing her the splendid, colourful decals he had been painstakingly pasting onto the pages of the ledger.

We all noticed at that time that Father had begun to shrink from day to day, like a nut drying out inside its shell.

This diminishment was by no means accompanied by any decline in his energies. On the contrary, the state of his health, humour, and mobility seemed to improve.

Now he would often cackle loudly and hysterically to himself, whooping with laughter; or else he would knock on the bed and answer 'Can I help you?' in various tones for hours on end. From time to time, he would slip out of bed, climb up onto one of the wardrobes, and squat there under the ceiling, arranging something in the dusty piles of junk.

Sometimes he set up two chairs opposite each other, hoisted himself up on their arms, and then rocked his legs backwards and forwards, his beaming eyes seeking signs of approval or encouragement in our faces. He seemed to have entirely reconciled himself with God. One night, the face of the bearded Demiurge appeared in the bedroom window, bathed in the dark purple of a Bengal light, gazing benignly at the sleeping figure of my father, whose melodious snoring seemed to wander across unknown regions of distant dream worlds.

During the long, gloomy afternoons of that late winter, Father would sometimes disappear for hours at a time into corners thickly piled with junk, feverishly searching for something.

More than once at dinner time, as we all sat down to the table, Father was absent. Mother would call out 'Jakub!' for a long time, tapping a spoon on the table, until finally he scrambled out of a wardrobe somewhere, covered in dust and cobwebs, his eyes distant and absorbed in complex matters known only to himself.

Sometimes he clambered up onto the curtain rail and struck a motionless pose mirroring the great stuffed vulture that hung on the wall on the other side of the window. He would remain frozen in that crouching position for hours on end, his eyes clouded over and a sly smile on his face, before suddenly flapping his arms like wings and crowing like a cock when somebody entered the room.

We ceased to pay any attention to these eccentricities, in which Father became ever more deeply entangled with each passing day. Almost entirely devoid of bodily needs, not eating for weeks at a time, he descended further into convoluted and bizarre affairs of which we had no understanding. Inaccessible to our arguments and pleas, he responded in snatches of his own inner monologue, whose flow could not be interrupted by anything outside it. Eternally preoccupied, feverishly animated, with a flush on his desiccated cheeks, he disregarded and ignored us.

We became accustomed to his harmless presence, to his quiet babbling, to the childish, self-absorbed chatter whose trills somehow resounded on the margins of our time. He would often vanish for days, disappearing somewhere into forsaken corners of the apartment, so that we could no longer find him.

Gradually these disappearances ceased to make any impression on us. We grew accustomed to them, and so when he reappeared many days later, a few inches shorter and thinner, his return was of little interest to us. We simply ceased to take him into account, so far had he strayed from everything human and real. Knot by knot, he broke loose from us; point by point, he dispensed with the ties that had bound him to the human community.

All that was left of him was a bit of bodily shell and a handful of absurd eccentricities. They too would disappear one day, as unremarked as the grey pile of rubbish in the corner that Adela swept up every morning and took out to the rubbish heap.

BIRDS

THEN CAME THE yellow days of winter, filled with boredom. The russet earth was covered with a worn tablecloth of snow, too short and filled with holes. There was not enough of it to cover all the roofs, which stood out black or rust-coloured, their shingled slopes and arches hiding the soot-coated spaces of attics beneath them: black, charred cathedrals, bristling with the ribs of rafters, purlins, and beams, the dark lungs of winter gales. Each new dawn exposed still more chimneys and roof vents that had sprouted overnight, blown up by the nocturnal gale like the black pipes of diabolical organs. The chimney sweeps could not get rid of the crows, which settled in the evening like black leaves on the branches of the trees by the church, and then flew off again in a flutter of wings before finally coming back to rest, each in its own place on its own branch. At dawn, they took off in great flocks, in clouds of coal dust, flakes of soot, billowy and fantastical, staining the cloudy yellow streaks of dawn with their restless cawing. The days hardened with cold and boredom, like last year's loaves of bread. We cut into them with blunt knives, without appetite, in a lazy stupor.

My father would no longer leave the house. He lit the stove and studied the unfathomable essence of fire, sniffing at the salty, metallic aftertaste and smoky aroma of the winter flames, as the cool caress of sala-manders licked the gleaming soot in the throat of the chimney. He lovingly carried out various repairs in the upper regions of the room. At all hours, he could be seen perched on top of a ladder, tinkering with some-thing by the ceiling, by the curtain rails, by the globes and chains of the hanging lamps. In the manner of a house painter, he used the ladder like a pair of enor-mous stilts, enjoying the bird's-eye view from up close to the painted sky, arabesques, and birds of the ceiling. He drifted ever further away from the practical affairs of everyday life. Whenever my mother, filled with care and concern for his condition, tried to coax him into a conversation about business or the payments due at the fast-approaching end of the month, he listened to her unheedingly, filled with anxiety, his distracted face wracked with convulsions. Sometimes he interrupted her suddenly with an imploring gesture, so as to dash off into the corner of the room, put his ear to a gap in the floor, and listen intently, index fingers raised to indicate the paramount importance of his investigations. Back then, we did not yet understand the sad background to these extravagances—the lamentable complex that was ripening in the depths.

My mother had no influence over him, and yet he accorded great veneration and attention to Adela. To Father, the cleaning of the room was now a great and important ritual, which he never failed to attend, following Adela's movements with a mixture of fear and shivers of pleasure. He ascribed to all her activities a deeper, symbolic meaning. When the girl swept the brush on its long rod across the floor with a bold, youthful motion, it almost overwhelmed him. Tears streamed from his eyes, his face was contorted with quiet laughter, and his body shuddered with the delicious spasm of orgasm. His ticklishness was heightened to the point of madness. It was enough for Adela to point her finger at him in a gesture vaguely suggestive of tickling for him to take off in a wild panic through the rooms of the house, slamming all the doors behind him and finally sprawling out on his stomach on the bed, writhing in convulsions of laughter under the influence of an internal image that he could not resist. In this way, Adela gained almost limitless power over Father.

It was around this time that we first noticed Father's passionate interest in animals. In the beginning, it was the passion of a hunter and artist rolled into one, perhaps accompanied by the deeper, zoological fellow feeling of a creature for related—albeit very different—forms of life, a kind of experimentation in as yet unprobed registers of being. Only later on did matters take the uncanny, sinful, and unnatural turn that it would perhaps be better not to bring to light here.

It started with a hatchery for bird eggs.

At great effort and expense, Father ordered pre-fertilized eggs from Hamburg, Holland, and African zoological stations, before giving them to enormous Belgian hens for incubation. The whole process was fascinating to me too, especially the hatching of the chicks: true freaks of nature in both form and colouration. It was impossible to discern the future peacocks, grouse, pheasants, and condors in those monsters, with their enormous, fantastical beaks, which gaped open as soon as they were born, hissing voraciously from the depths of their throats: lizards with the puny, naked bodies of hunchbacks. Placed in baskets filled with cotton wool, this dragon's litter lifted their blind, scaly heads on scrawny necks, squawking noiselessly from muted throats. My father walked among the shelves in a green apron, like a gardener among beds

of cacti, coaxing out of nothingness those blind bladders pulsing with life, those awkward bellies absorbing
the external world only in the form of food, those new
growths of life groping their way towards the light. A
few weeks later, when those blind buds of life had
burst into the light, the rooms of our apartment were
filled with a colourful murmur—the restless chirping
of their new inhabitants. They roosted all over the
curtain rails and the cornices of the wardrobes, nest-
ing in the thicket of tin branches and arabesques of a
multi-armed lamp hanging from the ceiling.

As my father studied his great ornithological
compendia, flicking through their colourful pages,
feathery phantasms seemed to flutter out of them, filling the room with a vibrant flapping in sheets of
purple and strips of sapphire, verdigris, and silver. At
feeding time, they formed a bright, rippling garden
bed on the floor, a living carpet that disintegrated
whenever someone carelessly stepped inside, dispersing into moving flowers that fluttered through the air
before finally settling over the upper regions of the
room. I distinctly recall one particular condor, an
enormous bird with a bare neck and wrinkled face
covered with exuberant growths. It was a scrawny
ascetic, a Buddhist lama, filled with imperturbable
dignity in its bearing, faithful to the rigid decorum of

its great lineage. When it sat opposite my father, motionless in the monumental pose of an ancient Egyptian deity, its eyes clouded over with a thin film that slid sideways over its pupils to seal it off in contemplation of its own stately solitude, it seemed in its stony profile to be my father's older brother. The same material of flesh, sinews, and tough, wrinkled skin; the same desiccated, bony face, with the same calloused, yawning eye sockets. Even the long, thin, gnarled hands of my father, with their overgrown fingernails, found their analogy in the talons of the condor. When I saw it asleep there, I could not fight off the impression of facing a mummy: the dried-out, shrunken mummy of my father. I believe this peculiar resemblance did not escape my mother's attention either, though we never broached the subject. Revealingly, the condor and my father used the same chamber pot.

Not content to stop at incubating ever new specimens, my father arranged avian nuptials in the attic. He sent out matchmakers, tethered enticing brides-to-be in the gaps and holes of the attic, and turned the enormous, gabled, shingled roof of our building into a veritable boarding house for birds, a Noah's ark to which all manner of winged beasts flocked from near and far. Even long after the final liquidation of the bird farm, this tradition of our home seemed to live on in the avian world, and the springtime migration often brought whole flocks of cranes, pelicans, peacocks, and all manner of other feathered creatures to our roof.

After a brief moment of splendour, the whole enterprise took a sad turn. For it soon became necessary to move Father into that junk-room part of the attic. At the crack of dawn, a confused clamour of avian voices reached us from above. The wooden soundboxes of the attic rooms echoed with soughing, fluttering, crowing, and gobbling, amplified by the natural resonance of the roof space. Father disappeared for several weeks. Only very seldom did he come down to the apartment, and then we noticed that he had grown smaller, thinner, and diminished. Sometimes, forgetting himself, he would leap up from his chair at the table, flap his arms like wings, and burst into a prolonged crowing, his eyes obscured by a cloudy film. Later, embarrassed, he would laugh along with us, trying to turn the whole incident into a joke.

Once, in the middle of her spring cleaning, Adela unexpectedly appeared in Father's bird kingdom. Standing in the doorway, she wrung her hands at the stench rising in the air and the piles of droppings heaped on the floors, tables, and furniture. With immediate resolve, she opened a window and drove the whole mass of birds into a tumultuous whirl with her long brush. A diabolical cloud of feathers, wings, and cries rose into the air, in the midst of which Adela—like a frenzied maenad veiled by her spinning thyrsus—danced her dance of destruction. Together with the flock of birds, my father flapped his wings in terror, trying desperately to lift himself up into the air. Slowly, the winged cloud dispersed, until at last only Adela was left on the battlefield, panting with exhaustion beside my father, whose face was forlorn and embarrassed, ready to accept any terms of capitulation.

A moment later, Father slunk down the stairs from his dominion: a broken man, a banished king who had lost his throne and his crown.

CINNAMON SHOPS

IN THE PERIOD of the shortest, sleepiest days of winter, hemmed in from both sides, morning and evening, by a furry margin of dusk, as the city branched out ever deeper into the labyrinths of winter nights, brought back to its senses only with an effort by the brief dawn, my father was already lost, sold, surrendered to the other sphere.

His face and head were wildly, luxuriantly overgrown with grey hair, which protruded unevenly in clumps, bristles, and long tufts that shot out of warts, eyebrows, and nostrils, giving his physiognomy the appearance of a bedraggled old fox.

His senses of hearing and smell had sharpened considerably, and it was clear from the twitching of his tense, silent face that he was in constant contact through these senses with an invisible world of dark recesses, mouse holes, musty crawl spaces, and chimney flues.

All the scratching and scrabbling of the night—that secret, creaking life of the floorboards—found in him a devotedly vigilant observer, spy, and co-conspirator. This absorbed him to such an extent that he became entirely immersed in that sphere, which remained inaccessible to us and which he did not seek to explain.

Many times, when the fooling of the invisible sphere had become too absurd, he just wagged his finger and chuckled to himself. Then he would exchange glances with the cat, who, likewise initiated into that world, would raise its cold, cynical, striped face, narrowing the slanting slits of its eyes with boredom and indifference.

Sometimes at dinnertime he suddenly put down his knife and fork in the middle of eating, got up in a feline motion, serviette still tied round his neck, tiptoed over to the door to the empty next room, and peeped through the keyhole with the utmost caution. Then he came back to the table, seemingly embarrassed, with an awkward smile on his face amidst the inarticulate mumbling and muttering of the internal monologue in which he was constantly engrossed.

In order to create a distraction and thus take him away from these unhealthy investigations, my mother would drag him out on evening walks, which he performed in silence, without resistance, but also without enthusiasm, preoccupied and absent in spirit. Once we even went to the theatre.

We found ourselves back in that large, poorly lit, dirty space, filled with a sleepy human hubbub and chaotic commotion. But once we had fought our way through the throng, the enormous pale blue curtain appeared before us, like the sky of some other firmament. Great masks, painted pink with bulging cheeks, wallowed in the vast expanse of cloth. That artificial sky billowed and expanded in all directions, swelling with the enormous breath of pathos and grand gestures, with the atmosphere of the artificial, dazzling world that would soon erect itself on the rumbling trestles of the stage. The shiver running through the great countenance of that sky—the breath of that enormous canvas from which the masks grew and came to life—exposed its illusory nature, creating that trembling of reality which we sense in metaphysical moments as the faint glimmer of the mystery.

The masks fluttered their red eyelids, whispering noiselessly with colourful lips, and I knew the moment was approaching when the tension of the mystery would reach its zenith and the swollen sky of the curtain would finally burst, rise, and reveal the most astonishing, extraordinary things.

But it was not given to me to witness that moment, as my father had begun in the meantime to betray signs of agitation, searching through his pockets and eventually declaring that he had forgotten his wallet, which contained money and important documents.

After a brief council with Mother, in which Adela's honesty was subjected to rapid scrutiny, it was proposed that I should set off home in search of the wallet. In Mother's opinion, there was still plenty of time before the show began and I was quick enough to make it back in time.

I stepped out into that winter night, resplendent with the illuminations of the sky. It was one of those bright nights in which the starry firmament expands and branches out, as if it had shattered, broken apart, and divided itself into a labyrinth of separate skies, enough of them to furnish a whole month of winter nights, covering all their nocturnal apparitions, adventures, disturbances, and carnivals with its silvery painted globes.

It is unforgivably reckless to send a young boy out on an urgent mission into such a night, for in its half-light the streets soon multiply, intertwine, and change places. The depths of the town open up to reveal double streets, doppelganger streets, false and misleading streets. The imagination, enchanted and deceived, creates illusory maps of the town, seemingly so familiar, on which the streets still have their old names and places, while the night in its inexhaustible fecundity has nothing better to do than to keep spinning out new and fanciful configurations. The temptations of winter nights usually begin innocently enough with the desire to take a shortcut via some unaccustomed passage or an untested side street. But on this occasion it all began rather differently.

After a few steps, I realized I had left my coat behind. I wanted to go back, but this seemed like an unnecessary waste of time, as the night was not at all cold—on the contrary, it was veined with streaks of a strange warmth, the breath of a false spring. The snow had shrunk into little white lambskins: sweet, innocent fleeces scented with violets. The sky had dissolved into the same little lambskins of clouds, while the moon seemed to multiply itself, displaying all its phases and positions at once.

The sky exposed its internal construction in multiple anatomical preparations, showing spirals and rings of light, cross sections of the pale-green substance of night, the plasma of the universe, the tissue of nocturnal reveries.

On such a night, one cannot walk along Rampart Street, or any of the other dark streets that form a kind of lining to the four sides of the market square, without recalling that at this hour the strange, alluring shops that one forgets on ordinary days are sometimes still open. I call them cinnamon shops, after the colour of the dark wood panelling inside them.

Those truly noble establishments, open late into the night, had always been the object of my most fervent desires.

Their poorly lit, solemn interiors were scented with the deep smell of paint, sealing wax, incense, and the aroma of faraway countries and rare materials. One could find Bengal lights, magic chests, stamps from countries long since vanished, Chinese decals, indigo, rosin from Malabar, eggs of exotic insects, parrots, toucans, live salamanders and basilisks, mandrake root, Nuremberg clocks, homunculi in flowerpots, microscopes and telescopes, and, above all, rare and peculiar books, old folios filled with strange drawings and astonishing tales.

I remember those dignified old merchants, serving their customers with lowered eyes, in discreet silence, filled with wisdom and understanding of the most secret desires. But above all there was one particular bookshop in which I had once viewed rare and forbidden prints, the publications of secret clubs, which lifted the veil on the most tormenting and intoxicating mysteries.

The chance to visit the shops came so seldom—and I even had a small but adequate sum of money in my pocket. Despite the importance of the mission entrusted to my zeal, I could not miss the opportunity.

According to my calculations, I would have to venture into a side street, and then pass two or three turnings to reach the street of the night shops. It would take me further away from my destination, but I could make up the time by coming back via the Saltworks Road.

Given wings by my desire to visit the cinnamon shops, I turned into a familiar street and flew more than walked, taking care not to lose my way. I soon passed the third or fourth turning, but still the street I sought had not arrived. What's more, even the configuration of the streets did not reflect my anticipated image of it. There was no sign of the shops. I walked along a street whose houses had no entrances—just windows shut tight, blinded by the glare of the moon. The right street must be on the other side of those houses, where the entrances are, I thought to myself. I anxiously quickened my pace, giving up in my heart on the thought of visiting the shops, if only I could get out of there back into a familiar part of town. I approached the end of the street, filled with apprehension as to where it might lead me. I came out onto a wide, sparsely built high street, very long and straight. At once, the fresh air of open space enveloped me. Along the street and buried in the gardens were pictur- esque villas, the ornate homes of the rich. Parks and orchard walls were visible in the gaps between them. From a distance, the scene reminded me of the lower, seldom visited parts of Lisznia Street. The light of the moon, diffused by thousands of cirrus clouds, like silver scales in the sky, was pale and bright as day. Only the parks and gardens were black in that silvery landscape.

After careful inspection of one of the buildings, I realized I was facing the rarely seen rear side of my school. I went to the door, which to my astonishment was open, with the entrance hall lit up. I stepped inside and found myself on the red carpet of a corridor. I hoped to creep through the building undetected and then exit by the front gate, thus making a considerable shortcut.

I recalled that at this hour Professor Arendt's after- school class would be in progress in his room, where we all gathered late into the night in the winter season, burning with a noble zeal for drawing exercises inspired by that extraordinary teacher.

Our little group of diligent pupils would almost be lost in the vast, dark room, while the shadows of our heads on the walls grew enormous, fracturing in the light of two small candles that burned in the necks of bottles.

In truth, we did not draw very much in those classes, and the professor was not rigorous in his demands. Some of us would even bring pillows from home and stretch out on the benches for a nap. Only the most conscientious among us would draw, huddling right under the candle in the golden circle of its light.

We often waited a long time for the professor to arrive, growing bored amidst sleepy conversation. Finally, the door would open and he would enter: small, with an exquisite beard, full of esoteric smiles, discreet silences, and the aroma of mystery. He shut the door quickly behind him, giving only a brief glimpse of his office: a throng of plaster shadows; classical fragments of pained Niobids, Danaids, and Tantalids; a sad and futile Olympus withering away in a plaster museum. The twilight of that room seemed to thicken, even during the day, sleepily overflowing with plaster dreams, empty looks, faded oval forms, and reveries retreating into nothingness. We sometimes liked to stand at the door listening to the silence, filled with the sighs and whispers of that crumbling heap of rubble amidst the cobwebs: a twilight of the gods disintegrating in boredom and monotony.

Filled with solemn dignity, the professor walked slowly between the empty benches and amongst the scattered little groups of pupils, as we sketched in the grey light of the winter's night. The atmosphere was cosy and somnolent. Here and there, some of my classmates would lie down to sleep. The candles burned out in their bottles. The professor delved into a voluminous book cabinet, filled with old folios, old-fashioned illustrations, etchings, and prints. With esoteric gestures, he showed us old lithographs of evening landscapes, nocturnal thickets, and park alleys in winter, blackening against the white paths of the moon.

Amidst our sleepy conversations, time flowed on imperceptibly and unevenly, forming strange knots in the passage of the hours or swallowing up whole intervals of its duration. Suddenly, without any transition, we found ourselves in a little gang already on our way home along a laneway white with snow, flanked by dry, black thickets of bushes. We walked along that shaggy verge of darkness, brushing against the bearskin of the bushes, which crackled under our feet in the bright, moonless night, long after midnight, like a false, milky day. The diffuse whiteness of the light reflecting off the snow from the pale air, from that milky expanse, was like the grey paper of an etching on which the deep black lines and hatchwork of the dense thickets had become entangled. Now, in its very depths, the night repeated that series of nocturnes, the night-time etchings of Professor Arendt, carrying on his fantasies.

In the black thicket of the park, in the shaggy hair of the bushes, amidst a mass of brittle brushwood, there were niches here and there, nests of the deepest, fluffiest blackness, full of tangled lines, secret gestures, disjointed conversations in sign language. It was snug and warm in those nests. We sat down in the soft, lukewarm snow in our shaggy coats, eating hazelnuts, which grew abundantly in the thicket in that springlike winter. Martens, weasels, and mongooses made their way through the bushes—furry, snuffling little animals, reeking of sheepskin, with their elongated bodies on stumpy legs. We suspected that some of them were exhibits from the school cabinet. Eviscerated and balding, they had sensed on that white night the voice of an old instinct in their empty insides, the voice of the rutting season, and were now returning to their dens for a short, illusory life.

Slowly the phosphorescence of the spring snow faded and flickered out, as the thick, black darkness before dawn came. Some of us fell asleep in the warm snow; others groped their way through the thicket to the doors of their homes, blindly stumbling into dark interiors, into the dreams of parents and brothers, into a deep snoring that they chased along belated paths.

Those night-time drawing sessions were so full of mysterious charm to me that I could not pass up the chance to look in briefly on the class, resolving that I would not be detained there for more than a moment. But as I climbed the cedar backstairs, filled with a sonorous resonance, I realized I was in a part of the building I had never visited before.

Not even the slightest sound disturbed the solemn silence. The corridors in this wing were more expansive, padded with plush carpets and filled with refinement. Little low-burning lamps shone at the corners. Turning one of them, I found myself in an even larger corridor, decorated with all the lavishness of a palace. One of its walls opened in wide, glass arcades into the interior of an apartment. From there, a long enfilade of rooms ran far into the distance, furnished with stunning opulence. My gaze followed a row of silk coverings, gilded mirrors, expensive furniture, and crystal chandeliers into the fluffy pulp of those sumptuous interiors, filled with a whirl of colours and shimmering arabesques, tangled garlands and budding flowers. The deep silence of those empty salons was filled only with the furtive looks exchanged by the mirrors and the panic of arabesques running in friezes high up across the walls, losing themselves in the mouldings of the white ceilings.

In reverence and awe, I stood before that splendour, suddenly comprehending that my nocturnal escapade had led me unexpectedly into the headmaster's wing, right to his private apartment. I stood nailed to the spot with curiosity, heart beating, ready to flee at the slightest stir. For how would I explain my nocturnal espionage and impudent inquisitiveness if they caught me here? The headmaster's young daughter might be sitting in one of those plush armchairs, quiet and unobserved, about to lift her eyes from her book—those black, sibylline, quiet eyes, whose gaze none of us could bear. But to turn back halfway, without executing my plan, seemed like cowardice. In any case, a deep silence held sway throughout those splendid interiors, illuminated by the muted light of the indefinite hour. Beyond the arcades of the corridor, I could see a large glass door leading out onto a terrace on the other side of an extensive drawing room. It was so quiet that I took heart. It did not seem so terribly risky now to descend the couple of steps down to the level of the room and then to cross the large, ornate rug in a few bounds to the terrace, from which I could easily get out onto the familiar street.

So that is what I did. Once I had descended onto the parquet floor of the drawing room, beneath large palms spreading out of their pots as high as the arabesques of the ceiling, I saw that I was already on neutral ground, since the drawing room had no front wall. It was, in fact, a kind of grand loggia connected by a few steps to a town square. It was almost like an offshoot of the square—some of the furniture even stood on the pavement. I skipped down a few stone steps and found myself back on the street.

The constellations hung steeply overhead; all the stars had revolved to the other side, but the moon, buried in a quilt of clouds illuminated by its unseen presence, seemed still to have an endless path before it, immersed in its intricate celestial procedures, with no thought of the dawn.

On the street, I made out the black shapes of a few droshky carriages, clapped-out and rickety like crippled, dozing crabs or cockroaches. A coachman leant down from his high box. He had a small face, ruddy and good-natured. 'Shall we go for a ride, young sir?' he asked. The carriage shivered in all the joints and sockets of its many-membered body, and then set off on light wheels.

But who on such a night would entrust himself to the whims of a droshky driver? Amidst the clatter of spokes and the thump of the carriage's body and hood, I could not agree on a destination with him.

He nodded perfunctorily and indulgently at everything I said, humming to himself as he drove us on a circuitous route around the town.

In front of a drinking den, we met a whole group of coachmen, who waved at the driver in friendly fashion. He answered them joyfully and then, without stopping the carriage, tossed the reins onto my lap, hopped down from the box, and joined the gang of his colleagues. The horse, a wise old carriage horse, looked around casually and carried on in its steady droshky trot. The horse somehow inspired confidence, seeming to be wiser than its driver. In any case, I did not know how to drive, so I had no choice but to surrender myself to its will. We drove into a suburban street lined on both sides with gardens. As we drove on, the gardens slowly gave way to parks, filled with tall trees, and then to forests.

I shall never forget that luminous ride on the brightest of winter nights. The colourful map of the heavens expanded into a measureless dome piled high with fantastical lands, oceans, and seas, marked with the lines of starry currents and eddies, the luminous lines of heavenly geography. The air became radiant and light to breathe, like silver gauze. It smelt of violets. Trembling anemones emerged from under white karakuls of woolly snow, holding sparks of moonlight in their delicate cups. The whole forest seemed to be illuminated with thousands of lights and stars, which the December firmament had poured down in floods. The air breathed with a kind of secret spring, an inexpressible purity of snow and violets. We drove into hilly terrain. The lines of the hills, shaggy with the naked branches of trees, rose up to the sky like blissful sighs. On those happy hillsides, I spotted groups of wanderers gathering fallen stars wet with snow amidst the moss and bushes. The road became steep; the horse began to slip, struggling to pull the carriage, which rattled in all its joints. I was happy. My lungs drew in the blissful spring of the air, the freshness of stars and snow. Under the horse's breast was a bank of white, snowy foam, which piled up higher and higher. The horse pushed laboriously through the pure fresh mass of it. Finally, he stopped. I got out of the carriage. He was panting heavily, his head hung low. I hugged his head to my chest, as tears glistened in his big, black eyes. Then I saw the round, black wound in his belly. 'Why didn't you tell me?' I whispered, sobbing. 'My dear, it was all for you,' he said, and then became very small, like a wooden toy. I left him. I felt strangely light and happy. I pondered whether to wait for the little local train that stopped there or to return to the town on foot. I began to descend by a steep, winding path through the forest—at first in a light, springy step, then gathering speed into a jaunty, happy run, which soon turned into a glide, as if I were skiing. I could regulate my speed at will, steering with the slightest turns of my body.

As I approached the town, I slowed my triumphal run, changing it into a respectable stroll. The moon still hung high above. The transformations of the sky—the metamorphoses of its many vaults into ever more masterful configurations—were endless. Like a silver astrolabe, the sky opened its internal mechanism on that magical night, revealing the gilded mathematics of its cogs and gears in infinite evolutions.

On the market square, I met some people taking a stroll. All of them, enchanted by the night's display, had their faces raised, silvery with the magic of the sky. Any concern for the wallet had left me entirely. My father, immersed in his various eccentricities, had no doubt forgotten its loss by now, and I did not care about Mother.

On such a night, unique in all the year, one is visited by happy thoughts, inspiration, and the prophetic touch of the finger of God. Filled with ideas and plans, I was about to head home when I happened upon my classmates out walking with their books under their arms. They had set off for school early, woken by the brightness of the night, which did not want to end.

We went for a stroll together along a steeply falling street scented with violets, unsure if it was still the magic of the night that shone silver on the snow or if the day was already dawning . . .

THE STREET OF
CROCODILES

M Y FATHER KEPT in the bottom drawer of his large desk an old and beautiful map of our town.

It was a whole folio volume of parchment pages, which had been stuck together with strips of canvas to create an enormous wall map in the form of a bird's-eye panorama.

Hung on the wall, it took up almost the entire space of the room, opening a wide view over the whole valley of the Tyśmienica River, which meandered in a wavy ribbon of pale gold: over a lake region of over-flowing swamps and ponds, over undulating foothills extending to the south, at first sparsely, and then in ever closer ranges, in a chessboard of rounded hills that grew smaller and paler as they receded into the golden, smoky mist of the horizon. From that faded distance of the periphery, the town emerged and swelled towards the middle ground, and then ever closer in indistinguishable complexes, in dense blocks and masses of houses, cut through with the deep ravines of the streets, until finally one could make out the individual tenement buildings, etched with the sharp distinctness of views seen through a telescope. In this foreground, the etcher had captured all the tangled and manifold tumult of the streets and alleyways, the sharp clarity of the cornices, architraves, and pilasters, glowing in the late, dark gold of a cloudy afternoon that had sunk all the niches and window recesses into the deep sepia of shadow. The lumps and prisms of that shadow cut into the canyons of the streets like dark honeycomb, plunging half a street here and an empty lot there into its warm, juicy mass, dramatizing and orchestrating that multiplicitous architectural polyphony in a gloomy romance of shadows.

On this map, made in the style of a baroque panorama, the district of the Street of Crocodiles shone with an empty whiteness of the colour used on geographical charts to mark the polar regions or unknown lands of uncertain existence. Only the lines of a few streets stood out in black, their names given in a simple, unadorned script in contrast with the ornate roman script calligraphy of the other names. The cartographer had apparently been reluctant to concede the connection of that district with the rest of the town, expressing his reservations through that distinct and disparaging style.

To fully comprehend these reservations, we must now turn our attention to the ambivalent and dubious nature of the district itself, so different in tone from the other parts of the town.

It was an industrial and commercial area, which garishly displayed its soberly utilitarian character. The general spirit of the age, with its mechanism of economics, had not spared our town either, putting down greedy roots on a patch of its peripheries and growing into a parasitical district there.

While an illicit, nocturnal trade, full of solemn ceremony, still held sway in the old town, the modern, sober forms of commercialism had developed rapidly in this new district. A pseudo-Americanism, grafted onto the stale old ground of the town, had shot up in a luxuriant but colourless vegetation of trashy, paltry pretentiousness. One saw cheap, shoddily constructed tenement buildings, their grotesque façades covered with monstrous mouldings and cracked stucco. Rickety old suburban houses had been hastily furnished with grand portals, which only on closer inspection were exposed as poor imitations of metropolitan amenities.

Flawed, murky windows that mirrored the dark image of the street in shimmering reflections; the rough sawn wood of the portals; the grey atmosphere of the barren interiors, filled with cobwebs and dust, which coated the high shelves and bare, crumbling walls—it all gave the shops the stamp of a wild Klondike. One after another, they lined up in rows down the street: tailor's shops, clothing stores, porcelain makers, chemists, and hairdressers. Their grey display windows flashed signs in gilded plastic letters running in semicircles or diagonal lines: CONFISERIE, MANICURE, KING OF ENGLAND.

The native residents of the town kept their distance from that neighbourhood, which was inhabited by rabble, riff-raff, creatures without character, without substance, the moral dregs, the trashy subspecies of human being that always arises in such ephemeral environments. But in days of dissipation, in hours of base temptation, it sometimes happened that one or another of the townsfolk would stray, half by accident, into that dubious district. Even the very best were not entirely immune to the temptations of voluntary degradation, a levelling of boundaries and hierarchies, a wallowing in the shallow mud of community, in easy intimacy and dirty intermingling. The district was an Eldorado for moral deserters, fugitives from the banner of their own dignity. Everything there seemed suspicious and ambivalent; everything was an invitation to impure desires, with a furtive wink, a cynically articulated gesture, a conspiratorial flash of the eyes; everything released base nature from its shackles.

The uninitiated could never quite put their finger on the strange peculiarity of that district: its lack of colour, as if in that trashy town, erected in haste, there had been no time for the luxury of colours. Everything there was grey, like the monochrome photographs of an illustrated brochure. This resemblance went beyond mere metaphor. Indeed, sometimes when one wandered through that part of the town, one had the impression of flicking through a brochure, through the dull copy of commercial advertising, among which various suspicious announcements, confidential memos, and dubious illustrations had parasitically taken root. And those wanderings turned out to be just as empty and futile as the excitation of fantasies inflamed by the pages and columns of pornographic publications.

One would enter a tailor's shop to order some clothes—clothes of the cheap elegance so characteristic of the district. The shop is large, empty, high-ceilinged, and drab. Enormous, multi-layered shelves rise up, one on top of another, into the indeterminate heights of the hall. The rows of empty shelves draw one's gaze up to the ceiling, which might just as well be the sky—the miserable, colourless, flaking sky of that district. Yet the storerooms visible through an open door are stacked high with boxes and cartons, piled up in an enormous filing system that disintegrates at the top, under the convoluted sky of the attic, and cascades down into an immense void, into the bare building blocks of nothingness. No light comes through the large grey windows, divided up into multiple squares like sheets of graph paper, as the space of the shop is already filled, like water, with an indifferent, grey glow that casts no shadows and illuminates nothing. Before long, a slender young man approaches us—obsequious, pliant, amenable—ready to fulfil our wishes and shower us with the cheap, facile blandishments of the sales assistant. But when he unfurls the enormous rolls of cloth—fitting, folding, draping the endless stream of material that flows through his hands, forming illusory frock coats and trousers from its waves as he chatters away—the whole manipulation seems somehow irrelevant, a sham, a comedy, a veil ironically flung over the true meaning of the matter.

The shop girls come and go, dark and slender, each with some flaw in her beauty (characteristic of this district of damaged goods), sometimes stopping in the storeroom doorway to see if the familiar business (confided to the experienced hands of the sales assistant) has reached the appropriate point. The sales assistant preens and fawns, at times giving the impression of a transvestite. One would like to grab him under the soft folds of his chin or pinch his pale, powdered cheek, as he discreetly turns one's attention with a conspiratorial look to the trademark of a product—a trademark bearing an obvious symbolism.

Slowly the business of choosing clothes fades into the background. That degenerate young man, soft to the point of effeminacy, full of understanding for the most intimate stirrings of the customer's desire, shuffles strange trademarks before his eyes, a whole library of trademarks, the display cabinet of a sophisticated collector. By then it has become apparent that the clothing shop was but a façade, behind which lies an antiquarian bookshop with a selection of highly dubious publications and private prints. The obsequious sales assistant opens up more storerooms, piled to the ceiling with books, drawings, and photographs. Those vignettes and drawings surpass even our wildest dreams a hundred times over. We had no inkling that such climaxes of degeneracy, such whimsies of debauchery, could exist.

The shop girls pass to and fro with ever greater frequency between the rows of books, grey and papery as prints, but filled with pigment in their degenerate faces—the dark pigment of brunettes in a shade of glossy, greasy black, which, hidden in the eyes, suddenly zigzags out of them in a shimmering, cockroachy flash. In blushing cheeks, in the piquant stigmata of moles, in the shameful signs of dark fluff, the race of a dark, rankling blood reveals itself. That excessively intense shade of colour, that thick and aromatic mocha, seems to tarnish the books that they take into olive hands. Their touch seems to stain them, leaving a dark rain of freckles in the air, a streak of tobacco, like a puffball with an arousing, animal scent. Meanwhile, the general dissolution has increasingly dispensed with even the appearance of propriety. The sales assistant, having exhausted his importunate activity, slowly slips into womanly passivity. Now he reclines on one of the many couches scattered about the area of books, revealing a feminine décolletage in silk pyjamas. Some of the shop girls demonstrate the figures and poses of various cover illustrations, while others doze on makeshift beds. The pressure on the customer is relaxed. He has been released from the centre of impertinent interest and left to his own devices. Busy in conversation, the shop girls pay no further attention to him. With their backs or sides to him, they freeze in arrogant new poses, shifting from foot to foot, tapping a flirtatious shoe, letting a serpentine shiver of limbs run up and down their slender bodies to besiege the aroused observer, whom they ignore. And so they seem to withdraw, slipping away with cold calculation into the depths and opening a free space for the guest's own initiative. Let us seize this moment of inattention to escape the unpredictable consequences of that innocent visit and retreat back onto the street.

Nobody stops us. Through corridors of books, past long shelves of periodicals and publications, we exit the shop, and then suddenly here we are in the part of the Street of Crocodiles where an elevated point offers a view over almost the entire length of its wide thoroughfare, as far as the distant, unfinished buildings of the train station. It's a grey day, as always in that district, and the whole scene resembles a photograph from an illustrated magazine, so grey and flat are the houses, people, and vehicles. Reality is as thin as paper, betraying its imitative nature in all its cracks. At times, one has the impression that only in the small patch immediately in front of us does it all come together in exemplary fashion into the pointillized image of a metropolitan boulevard, while on the edges the whole improvised masquerade dissolves and disintegrates, incapable of keeping up its role, until finally it falls apart behind us into plaster and oakum, the junk room of an enormous empty theatre. The tension of the pose, the artificial gravity of the mask, an ironic pathos tremble on that surface.

But we are far from desiring to unmask the spectacle. Against our better judgement, we feel ourselves being drawn into the trashy charm of the district. After all, the image of the town does not lack a certain sense of self-parody. The rows of small, single-storey suburban houses shift into multi-storied tenement buildings, which, seemingly built from cardboard, form a conglomerate of signboards, blank office windows, glassy grey displays, advertisements, and street numbers. Under the buildings, the river of the crowd flows on. The street is as wide as a metropolitan boulevard, but the roadway, like a village square, is made of compacted clay, filled with potholes, puddles, and grass. The street traffic of the district suggests various comparisons in this spot; the inhabitants speak of it with pride and a conspiratorial gleam in their eye. The grey, impersonal crowd is absorbed in its role, filled with zeal in its performance of metropolitan appearances. Yet in spite of the hustle and bustle, one has the impression of an errant, monotonous, aimless wandering, a dreamy procession of marionettes. An atmosphere of strange triviality permeates the whole scene. The crowd flows on monotonously, and one somehow sees it indistinctly, the figures flowing by in a gentle, tangled tumult, without ever fully coming into focus. Sometimes from that hubbub of many heads, we pick out a dark, living glance, a black bowler hat pulled down over a head, half a face split by a smile, with lips that have just said something, a leg extended in a step now frozen forever.

A peculiar feature of the district are the driverless droshky carriages running wild through the streets. Not that there is any shortage of droshky drivers here, but they are mixed in with the crowd and preoccupied with a thousand other matters, not bothering with their carriages. In this district of appearances and empty gestures, nobody puts much stock in the precise destination of a carriage ride, and the passengers entrust themselves to these errant vehicles with the reckless abandon that defines everything here. One can often see them on dangerous corners, leaning out of a rickety cabin with reins in hand, as they perform a difficult overtaking manoeuvre.

We also have trams in that district. The ambition of the town councillors here celebrates its greatest triumph. Yet the sight of those wagons is pitiable— made from papier mâché, with walls bent and crumpled from many years of use. They are often missing their front walls, so that one can see the passengers inside, seated stiffly, comporting themselves with the greatest dignity. The trams are pushed along by the town porters. But the strangest thing on the Street of Crocodiles is the railway line.

At irregular hours, usually towards the end of the week, one sometimes sees a crowd of people waiting at a street corner for the train. Nobody is ever sure if it will come or where it will stop, and it often happens that people line up in two different spots, unable to agree on the stopping place. They wait a long time, standing in a black, silent throng along the barely drawn tracks of the line, their faces in profile like a row of pale paper masks, cut out into a fantastical line of stares. At last, the train arrives, unexpectedly emerging from a side street where nobody was waiting, flat as a snake, tiny, with a small, squat, puffing locomotive. It pulls into that black lane, darkening the street as the row of its carriages spreads clouds of coal dust. The dark puffing of the steam engine and an air of strange solemnity, filled with a sadness stifled by haste and irritation, momentarily turns the street into the hall of a train station in the swiftly falling winter dusk.

Speculation on train tickets and bribery are a plague in our town.

At the last moment, with the train already waiting in the station, negotiations with the corrupt officials of the railway company are conducted in nervous haste. Before they can conclude, the train sets off again, accompanied by the slow-moving, disappointed crowd, which follows it some way before finally dispersing.

Narrowed for a moment into that improvised train station, filled with darkness and the excitement of faraway places, the street then becomes light again, widening and letting the carefree, monotonous crowd of strollers back through its channel to wander amidst the hubbub of conversation, past the shop displays — those dirty, grey quadrilaterals, filled with trashy goods, great wax mannequins, and hairdressers' dummies.

Prostitutes walk by, provocatively dressed in long, lacy dresses. In fact, they may be the wives of hairdressers or coffeehouse bandmasters. They walk with a predatory, swaggering step, their rotten, unwholesome faces all marked with a slight flaw to distinguish them: some squint with black, crooked eyes; others have a cleft lip, or are missing the tip of their nose.

The denizens of the town are proud of the odour of corruption emanating from the Street of Crocodiles. 'We don't want for anything here,' they observe proudly. 'We too can afford the real metropolitan debauchery.' They claim that every woman in the district is a coquette. Indeed, it is enough to look at one of them, and immediately you are met with that insistent, clinging look that freezes you with delightful certainty. Even the schoolgirls wear their hair ribbons in a characteristic way here, planting their slender legs in a peculiar style, with an impure flaw in their glance that prefigures future corruption.

And yet—and yet, are we now to betray the final mystery of that district, the carefully hidden secret of the Street of Crocodiles?

On several occasions in the course of our report, we have set down certain warning signs, giving subtle expression to our reservations. The attentive reader will not, then, be unprepared for the final turn of events. We have spoken already of the imitative, illusory nature of the district, but these words have a meaning too definitive and categorical to capture the partial and undecided nature of its reality.

Our language lacks expressions capable of measuring out the degree of reality, or of capturing its density. So let us say it without holding back: the curse of that district is that nothing in it comes to fruition; nothing reaches its *definitivum*. All movements, once begun, hang suspended in mid-air; all gestures prematurely exhaust themselves, unable to pass a certain dead point. We have already noted the great extravagance and prodigality of intentions, projects, and expectations so characteristic of the district. The whole neighbourhood is nothing other than a fermentation of desires, prematurely unleashed, and thus impotent and empty. In an atmosphere of excessive permissiveness, the flimsiest fancy blooms, a momentary tension puffs up and sprouts into an empty, swollen growth, shooting out the fine grey vegetation of fluffy weeds and colourless, hairy poppies made of the delicate tissue of hallucination and hashish. The idle, dissolute fluid of sin hangs over the whole district, where houses, shops, and people sometimes seem to be but a shiver on its feverish body, the goosebumps on its febrile dreams. Nowhere else do we feel so threatened by possibilities, shaken by the nearness of fulfilment, pale and numb with the delicious terror of consummation. But this is not the end of it.

After passing a certain point of tension, the flow stops and reverses, the atmosphere fades and decays, the possibilities wither and disintegrate into nothingness, and the frenzied grey poppies of excitation scatter into ash.

We will forever regret leaving that clothes shop of ill repute. We will never find our way back to it again. And so we will roam from signboard to signboard, losing our way hundreds of times. We will visit dozens of storerooms, perhaps finding very similar ones, wandering among rows of books and flipping through magazines and prints, having long, roundabout conversations with shop girls, with their excessive pigment and flawed beauty, incapable of comprehending our wishes.

We will become entangled in misunderstandings, until at last all our fervour and arousal will evaporate in futile exertions, in a hopeless pursuit to no avail.

All our hopes were a misunderstanding; the ambivalent look of the shop and its staff were an illusion. The garments were real garments, and the sales assistant had no hidden intentions. The women's world of the Street of Crocodiles was marked by an entirely second-rate corruption, padded by thick layers of moral prejudice and banal vulgarity. In this town of cheap human material, there was no extravagance of instinct or dark, unusual passions.

The Street of Crocodiles was our town's concession to modernity and metropolitan corruption. Apparently we could afford nothing better than a paper imitation, a photomontage of clippings from last year's stale newspapers.

COCKROACHES

I T WAS THE time of grey days that followed the splendid colours of my father's age of genius. These were long weeks of depression, heavy weeks without Sundays or holidays, with a closed sky and an impoverished landscape. By then, Father was no longer with us. The upper rooms had been cleaned out and let to a certain telephonist. Of the bird farm, only a single specimen remained: a stuffed condor standing on a shelf in the living room. In the cool semi-darkness of the drawn net curtains, it stood there, as it once had in life, on one leg, in the pose of a Buddhist sage, its bitter, withered face like that of an ascetic, petrified into an expression of utter indifference and abnegation. Its eyes had fallen out, and sawdust seeped through its teary sockets. Only the horny Egyptian growths on its great, bare beak and on its bald neck—growths and protuberances of a faded blue colour—conferred on that senile head something honourably hieratic.

Its feathery habit had been eaten through in many places by moths, and it had lost the soft grey feathers that Adela had swept up once a week with the anonymous dust of the room. In the bald spots, a thick burlap canvas showed through, shedding tufts of hemp. In private, I resented Mother for the ease with which she had shaken off the loss of Father. She had never loved him, I thought, and since Father was not planted in the heart of any woman, then he could not take root in reality, and thus he was doomed to float eternally on the periphery of life, in half-real regions, on the margins of reality. He had not even earnt an honest, civic death, I thought; everything had to be strange and dubious with him. I decided to ambush Mother with an open conversation on the subject at an opportune moment. That day (a heavy winter's day on which the soft down of dusk had been falling since morning), my mother had a migraine and was lying on the sofa by herself in the living room.

Since Father's disappearance, an exemplary order had reigned in that seldom visited, ceremonial room, tended by Adela with her wax and brushes. The furniture was draped with covers; all the appliances had submitted to the iron discipline that Adela imposed. Only a bunch of peacock's feathers in a vase on the dresser could not be kept in check. They remained a

frivolous, dangerous element, with a vague air of revolution about them, like a rowdy class of middle-school
girls, full of piety in their eyes and debauched frivolity
behind them. Those eyes stared out all day long, drill-
ing holes in the walls: winking, crowding together, fluttering their eyelids with fingers on lips, filled with
pranks and giggles. They filled the room with chatter
and whispers that scattered like butterflies about the
multi-armed lamp, slapping in a colourful crowd into
the matte surfaces of the senile mirrors—no longer
accustomed to such movement and merriment—or
peeping through the keyholes. Even in the presence of
my mother, who lay on the sofa with her head wrapped
up, they could not restrain themselves; they winked at
one another, sending signals and communicating in a
mute, colourful alphabet filled with secret meanings. I
was irritated by their scornful conspiring and restless
plotting behind my back. With my knees pressed up
against Mother's sofa, inspecting the delicate material
of her dressing gown with two fingers as if lost in
thought, I said with a casual air: 'I've wanted to ask
you for ages: is it really him?' And though I did not
indicate the condor, even with a glance, my mother
guessed at once and became confused, lowering her
eyes. I deliberately allowed a moment to pass, so as to
relish her confusion. Then, controlling my rising

anger, I asked calmly: 'So what is the meaning of all the gossip and lies you are spreading about Father?'

But her face, which had at first fallen into a panic, soon began to compose itself again. 'What lies?' she asked, blinking her eyes, which were empty and swollen a dark blue colour, with no whites visible. 'I've heard them from Adela,' I said. 'But I know they come from you. I want to know the truth.'

Her mouth trembled delicately; her pupils, avoiding my glance, slipped into the corners of her eyes. 'I didn't lie,' she said, her lips swelling and shrinking all at once. I felt that she was flirting with me, like a woman with a man. 'With the cockroaches, it's true—I mean, you remember it yourself . . .' She became confused again. I did indeed remember the invasion of cockroaches, the deluge of their black swarm, filling the darkness of the night with a spidery hustle. All the cracks were filled with twitching antennae; every crevice could suddenly shoot out a cockroach; every gap in the floor could hatch that black lightning to flash across the room in a frenzied zigzag. Ah, that wild insanity of panic, written in shining black lines over the chalkboard of the floor. Ah, Father's screams of terror, as he leapt from chair to chair with a javelin in his hand. Refusing both food and drink, the flush of fever upon his cheeks and a spasm of disgust etched around his mouth, my father ran completely wild. It was clear that no human body could withstand the tension of such hatred for long. A terrifying repulsion had turned his face into a frozen, tragic mask, in which only his pupils, hidden beneath his lower eyelids, were on the lookout, taut as bowstrings in eternal apprehension. With a wild shriek, he would suddenly spring up from his seat and fly blindly into a corner of the room, raising his javelin, on which an enormous cockroach was impaled, waving its tangled legs in desperation. Adela would come to his aid, pale with terror as he was, taking the lance away from him together with the impaled trophy, which she drowned in a wooden pail.

But even back then I could not say for sure if Adela's tales had implanted these images in my mind or if I had witnessed them myself. My father did not then possess the power of immunity that protects healthy people from the fascination of disgust. Instead of separating himself from the terrible magnetic force of that fascination, my father, now prey to madness, became more and more entangled in it. The sad consequences did not take long to reveal themselves. The appearance of the first suspicious signs filled us with horror and sadness. Father's behaviour changed. His earlier frenzy and the euphoria of his excitement faded. His movements and facial expressions began to betray signs of a guilty conscience. He began to avoid us. He hid all day long in corners, in cupboards, under the duvet. More than once, I saw him staring at his own hands, deep in contemplation, examining the consistency of his skin and nails, on which black stains were beginning to appear, like the scales of a cockroach.

During the day, he still resisted with the last of his strength, fighting valiantly, but at night the fascination assailed him in fearful attacks. I saw him late at night in the light of a candle on the floor. He was lying there naked, speckled with the black stains of the totem, the lines of his ribs showing through in a fantastical tracing of his anatomy. He was crouched on all fours, demented by the fascination of an aversion that had dragged him far along its twisted paths. He moved in a complicated, multi-limbed motion in which I recognized with horror the imitation of some cockroachy ceremony.

From then on, we disowned Father. His resemblance to a cockroach became more and more pronounced by the day—my father was turning into a cockroach.

We soon became accustomed to it. We saw him ever more seldom; for weeks at a time, he would disappear off somewhere on his cockroachy paths. We ceased to differentiate him from them as he merged completely with that uncanny black tribe. Who could say if he was still alive somewhere in a crack in the floor, if he was running through the rooms at night, engrossed in cockroachy affairs, or if he was among those dead insects that Adela found each morning, lying with bellies up and legs bristling, to be swept up into the dustpan and tossed away?

'And yet,' I said, disconcerted, 'I'm certain that the condor is him.' Mother looked at me from under her eyelashes. 'Don't torment me, darling. I've told you already that Father is travelling around the country as a salesman. You know very well that he sometimes comes home at night only to leave before dawn for distant parts.'

THE GALE

I N THAT LONG, empty winter, darkness in our town yielded an enormous, hundredfold harvest. For too long, the attics and junk rooms had not been cleaned; pots were piled on top of pots, flasks over flasks, and empty batteries of bottles were allowed to multiply endlessly.

Up there, in those burnt-out, many-beamed forests of attics and roofs, the darkness began to degenerate and ferment wildly. And so began those black parliaments of pots, those garrulous and empty assemblies, that raucous flasking, with the gurgling of bottles and cans. Until one night, from under those shingled expanses, the phalanxes of pots and flasks formed up and surged out in a great jostling crowd into the town.

Attics upon attics expanded out of one another and shot out in black rows; through their spacious echoes ran cavalcades of beams and girders, the simpering of wooden trestles knelt down on knees of fir, until at last they burst out into freedom to fill the expanses of the night with the galloping of rafters and a tumult of purlins and collar beams.

Those black rivers overflowed in rushing currents of barrels and cans that poured through the nights. Their glossy black, clamorous ranks lay siege to the town. For nights on end, that dark, teeming hubbub of vessels advanced like armies of chattering fish, an irrepressible invasion of babbling pails and backtalking tubs.

Hammering with their bottoms, the buckets, barrels, and jugs piled up high; the clay vats of stove-fitters dangled in the air; the old caps and top hats of dandies clambered on top of one another, rising into the sky in tall columns that then fell apart.

All the while, they clumsily rattled the pegs of their wooden tongues, jabbering out a gibberish of curses and insults, spitting out mud from their wooden snouts over the whole expanse of the night. Until at last they had cursed and blasphemed their way to their end.

Summoned by that gossiping babble of containers, which had fanned out in all directions, the great caravans and trains of the gale finally arrived to loom over the night. An enormous encampment—a black, mobile amphitheatre—descended in mighty circles on the town. The darkness exploded in an immense and turbulent gale, which raged for three days and three nights . . .

*

'You won't be going to school today,' said Mother in the morning. 'There's a terrible gale outside.' Inside the room, a delicate veil of smoke rose into the air, smelling of resin. The stove whistled and howled, as if a pack of dogs or demons were tethered inside it. The great daub painted on its pot belly twisted itself into a colourful grimace, fantasticizing with its cheeks puffed out.

I ran barefoot to the window. The length and breadth of the sky was swollen with the winds. Silvery white and spacious, it was covered with force lines strained to breaking point and grim furrows like frozen veins of tin or lead. Carved up into energy fields and trembling with the tension, it was filled with latent dynamism. Inscribed into it were the diagrams of the gale, which—invisible and ineffable—loaded the landscape with its power.

It could not be seen. But it made itself known by the houses and roofs into which it poured its fury. One after another, the attics seemed to swell and explode in a frenzy when its power entered them.

It cleaned out the squares, leaving a white void behind it on the streets; it swept clear the whole expanse of the market square. Only here and there, bowed beneath it and flapping in its gusts, a solitary person remained, clinging onto the corner of a house. The whole market square seemed to bulge and gleam like a bald patch under its powerful flights.

Up in the sky, the wind blew cold, dead colours: streaks of verdigris, yellow, and lilac; the distant vaults and arcades of its labyrinth. Beneath those skies, the roofs stood black and misshapen, filled with impatience and expectation. Those the gale had entered swelled with inspiration, towering above the neighbouring houses and hurling out prophecies into the tempestuous sky. Before long, they faltered and collapsed, no longer able to contain the powerful breath that blew through them to fill the expanse with tumult and terror. Then other houses rose instead with a roar, portending in paroxysms of clairvoyance.

The enormous beech trees around the church stood with raised arms, like witnesses to shocking revelations, screaming and screaming.

Further on, beyond the roofs of the market square, I saw the distant firewalls and naked gable ends of the suburbs. They clambered on top of one another and expanded, stiff and dumbstruck with terror. A cold, faint, red glow tinged them with late colours.

We did not eat dinner that day, as the stove belched clouds of smoke into the kitchen. The rooms were cold and smelt of the wind. At around two o'clock in the afternoon, a fire broke out in the suburbs and spread rapidly. Mother and Adela began to pack our bedding, furs, and valuables.

Night came. The gale increased in strength and fury, growing to engulf the whole expanse. Now it no longer visited the houses and roofs, but built a multi-storied, manifold expanse above the town—a black labyrinth rising up in infinite layers. From that labyrinth, it shot out whole galleries of rooms, erected wings and annexes in flashes of lightning, rolled out long enfilades with a rumble, and then allowed these imagined vaults, stories, and casemates to collapse, while it soared still higher, shaping the formless expanse with its own inspiration.

The room shook and the paintings on the walls rattled. The windowpanes gleamed in the greasy glow of the lamp. The curtains on the window hung bloated with the breath of that stormy night. We suddenly realized that nobody had seen Father all day. He must have gone out early in the morning to the shop, we surmised, where the gale had taken him by surprise and blocked his return.

'He hasn't eaten anything all day,' bemoaned Mother. One of the more senior shop assistants, Teodor, agreed to venture out into the night, into the gale, to take him some food. My brother joined the expedition.

Wrapped up in great bearskins, they filled their pockets with clothes irons and kitchen mortars as ballast to stop the gale from carrying them away.

Cautiously they opened the front door. No sooner had the shop assistant and my brother set foot out into the darkness than the night swallowed them up on the very threshold of the house. The gale swept away every trace of their exit in an instant. Not even the torch they had taken with them could be seen through the window.

After devouring them, the gale abated for a moment. Adela and Mother tried to light the fire in the stove again. The matches went out, while ash and soot blew out onto the floor. We stood at the door and listened. In the lamentations of the gale, one could hear all manner of voices, exhortations, entreaties, and tales. It seemed to us that we could hear Father's cries for help as he blundered through the gale, and then my brother and Teodor casually nattering outside the front door. The impression was so deceptive that Adela opened the door, and there indeed were Teodor and my brother, emerging with a struggle from the gale in which they were immured up to their armpits.

They came breathlessly into the entrance hall, closing the door behind them with an effort. For a moment they had to lean against it, so powerfully did the gale besiege the entrance. At last, they drove home the bolt, and the wind raced off somewhere else.

They told us confusedly about the night and the gale. Their bearskins, saturated with the wind, now smelt of the air. They fluttered their eyelids in the light, while their eyes, still filled with the night, leaked darkness with every beat of their lashes. They had not been able to reach the shop; they had lost their way and barely made it back. They could not recognize the town, whose streets had all been shifted around.

Mother suspected they were lying. Indeed, the whole scene gave us all the impression that they had been standing outside in the darkness for that quarter of an hour, without going anywhere. Or perhaps the town and the market square were no longer there, and only the gale and the night now surrounded our house, like the dark wings of a backstage filled with howls, whistles, and moans. Perhaps the vast, lamentable spaces suggested by the gale were not there at all; perhaps those pitiful labyrinths, the many-windowed wings and corridors on which the gale played—as if on long black flutes—were not there either. We grew increasingly convinced that the whole storm was but a nocturnal quixotism, imitating in the narrow confines of those backstage wings the tragic expanses, cosmic homelessness and orphanhood of the gale.

The door to the entrance hall opened ever more frequently to admit guests wrapped up in shawls and mantles. A panting neighbour or friend slowly excavated himself from under coats and scarves, breathlessly spilling out stories and disjointed, muddled words that fantastically magnified the exaggerated expanse of the night. We all sat in the brightly lit kitchen. Beyond the hearth and the wide black hood of the chimney, a few steps led up to the attic door.

On these steps sat Teodor, listening as the gale played in the attic. In brief respites, he heard how the bellows of the attic's ribs folded up and the roof went limp, hanging there like giant lungs from which the air has escaped, only to catch its breath again and reconfigure itself into palisades of rafters, swelling like Gothic vaults and expanding in a forest of beams, filled with myriad echoes and booming like the body of an enormous double bass. But then we forgot about the gale. Adela ground cinnamon in a sonorous mortar. Aunt Perazja came to visit. Diminutive, bustling, and prudent, with a shawl of black lace over her head, she began to busy herself about the kitchen, helping Adela. Adela was plucking a rooster. Aunt Perazja lit a handful of papers under the chimney hood, and soon the broad streaks of flame were leaping up into its black mouth. Adela seized the rooster by the neck and held it over the flames to burn off the rest of the feathers. Suddenly the rooster flapped its wings in the fire, crowed noisily, and went up in flames. Aunt Perazja began to quarrel, curse, and swear. Shaking with fury, she threatened Adela and Mother with her fists. I could not understand what she was talking about as she grew more and more incandescent with anger, transforming into a hot ball of gesticulations and curses.

In this paroxysm of rage, it seemed she might gesticulate herself into pieces, falling apart, disintegrating, and dispersing into a hundred spiders that would scatter across the floor in a black, shimmering flight of frenzied, cockroachy movement. Instead, she began to diminish and shrink, still shaking and hurling out curses. Suddenly she waddled off, stooped and small, into the corner of the kitchen, where we kept the firewood, and began to sift feverishly through the resonant wood, cursing and coughing, until she found two slender, yellow splinters. She seized them in hands still trembling with outrage, and tried them on her feet. Then she climbed up onto them like stilts and began to walk about on those yellow crutches, clattering over the floorboards as she ran to and fro, faster and faster, along the sloping line of the floor. She leapt up onto a fir bench and hobbled along its rattling boards, and from there up onto a shelf of plates—a sonorous, wooden shelf running all the way around the kitchen—where she shuffled along on her crutch-stilts until finally, somewhere in a corner, getting smaller and smaller, she turned black and shrivelled like a burnt piece of paper, withered into a flake of ash, and then crumbled into dust and nothingness.

We all stood helplessly by in the face of that frenzied fury, which consumed and devoured itself. With sorrow, we watched the sad course of that paroxysm, and then, with a certain relief, returned to our own activities once the whole lamentable process had reached its natural conclusion.

Adela rang out on the mortar again as she ground the cinnamon; Mother picked up her interrupted conversation; and the shop assistant, Teodor, still listening to the prophecies of the attic, pulled funny faces, raising his eyebrows and chuckling to himself.

THE NIGHT OF THE
GREAT SEASON

Everyone knows that even in the run of ordinary, normal years, the eccentricity of time sometimes gives birth to other years: peculiar, degenerate years, which shoot out—like a sixth finger—a false, thirteenth month.

We call it false because it seldom reaches full maturity. Like children begotten too late, it remains retarded in its growth, a hunchback month, an offshoot, half withered and more imagined than real.

The summer's senile incontinence is to blame—its debauched, late vitality. It sometimes happens that August has passed, but the thick old trunk of the summer keeps producing out of sheer force of habit, punching out of its rotting wood those wild shoot days, weed days, barren and moronic, sometimes throwing in for good measure corncob days, empty and inedible—white, surprised, and superfluous days.

They grow, uneven and irregular, deformed and knitted together, like the fingers of a monstrous hand, budding and curling up into the shape of a fig.

Others compare those days to apocrypha secretly inserted between the chapters of the great tome of the year, to palimpsests furtively slipped between its pages, or to those blank, unprinted pages on which one's eyes, sated with reading and filled with content, begin to leak images and lose their colours, becoming paler and paler, reposing on the nothingness of those empty pages, before being dragged back into the labyrinths of new adventures and chapters.

Ah, that old, yellowed romance of the year—the vast, disintegrating tome of the calendar! It lies forgotten somewhere in the archives of time, where its content continues to grow between its covers, swelling ceaselessly with the garrulousness of the months, with the spontaneous generation of nonsense, with the tattle and dreams that multiply within it. And as I record these tales of ours, composing these stories about my father in the worn-out margins of its text, do I not surrender to the cheap hope that they will one day grow imperceptibly into the yellowed leaves of that most splendid, disintegrating tome, that they will enter into the great rustle of its pages as it devours them?

What we will speak of here took place in that thirteenth, supernumerary, false month of the year—on those dozen or so empty pages of the great chronicle of the calendar.

The mornings were strangely pungent and invigorating. The calmer, cooler tempo of time, the entirely new scent of the air, and the altered consistency of the light all told us that we had entered a different run of days, a new region of the Lord's Year.

One's voice quavered under those new skies as freshly and sonorously as in a brand-new, still empty apartment, filled with the scent of varnish, paint, and things begun but not yet put into use. With strange emotion, one tested the new echo, curiously slicing into it as one might cut into a coffee cake on a cool, sober morning the day before a journey.

My father was seated once again at the back counter of the shop in a small, vaulted room divided up like a beehive into multi-chambered filing cabinets, with endlessly peeling layers of papers, letters, and invoices. Out of the rustle of reports and the constant shuffle of papers, the square-ruled, empty existence of that room grew. From the ceaseless rearranging of files, an apotheosis of company letterheads reassembled itself in the air in the form of a factory town seen from above, bristling with smoking chimneys, surrounded by rows of medals, and lined with the curlicues and flourishes of pompous *& Co.*'s.

There sat Father, as if in an aviary, on a tall stool, while the dovecotes of filing cabinets rustled with papers and all the nests and holes were filled with the chirping of figures.

The depths of the vast shop were darkening, growing richer by the day in their stock of textiles, cheviots, velvets, and corduroys. On dark shelves, in those granaries and junk rooms of cool, felt hues, the dark, matured colour of things yielded a hundredfold interest, multiplying and sating the mighty capital of autumn. There that capital grew, darkening and expanding over the shelves, as if through the galleries of some enormous theatre, replenishing and multiplying itself each morning with new loads of merchandise, which groaning, bearded porters hauled in on bearish shoulders in boxes and packages amidst a haze of autumn freshness and vodka mingled with the morning chill. The shop assistants unloaded these new supplies of nourishing silk colours, meticulously stuffing all the holes and gaps of the high cabinets full of them. It was an enormous register of all the colours of the autumn, arranged in layers and sorted into shades that ran up and down, as if over sonorous steps, over scales of all the octaves of colour. It began at the bottom, timidly and plaintively sounding the alto of faded half-tones, then shifting into the bleached ashes of dahlia, into Gobelins greens and blues, swelling towards the heights in ever wider chords until it reached the navy blues, the indigo of distant forests, the plush of rustling parks, rushing through all the ochres, sanguines, russets, and sepias into the whispering shadow of withered gardens, and finally reaching the dark odour of mushrooms, the breath of rotting wood in the depths of the autumn night, and the dull accompaniment of the darkest basses.

My father walked along the arsenals of that autumn of cloth, calming and quieting their masses, their gathering power, the placid might of the Season. He wished to keep those reserves of stored colours intact for as long as possible. He was afraid to break that autumn endowment fund to exchange it for hard currency. But he knew, or sensed, that the time would come when the autumn gale—a wild, warm gale— would blow through those cabinets, that they would break open, and that nothing could stop the flood from bursting in streams of colour over the whole town.

The time of the Great Season was approaching. The streets came to life. At six o'clock in the evening, the town was blooming with fever, the houses were flushed, and people wandered about animated by some inner fire, garishly rouged and made-up, eyes glistening with a festive, beautiful, yet ill-omened ague.

On side streets and quiet backstreets leading out into an evening district, the town was empty. Only the children played on little squares under balconies—playing breathlessly, noisily, nonsensically. They put little bladders to their mouths, inflated them, and then suddenly puffed up like turkeys into great gobbling, spluttering growths, or transformed themselves into stupid rooster's masks, red and crowing, into colourful autumn monsters, fantastical and absurd. Swollen and crowing, it seemed they were about to rise into the air in long, colourful chains, spreading out over the town like formations of autumn birds, fantastical flotillas made of crêpe paper and the autumn weather. Or else, amidst shouts, they pushed one another along on clattering little carts, which rang out with a colourful rattle of wheels, spokes, and shafts. Loaded with their cries, the carts rolled down to the bottom of the street, as far as the low, swollen course of the evening river, where they fell apart into a wreckage of rollers, dowels, and sticks.

And while the children's games became ever more raucous and confused, the blushes of the town darkened and bloomed in purple. Suddenly the world began to wither and blacken, rapidly secreting from itself a hallucinatory dusk that infected all things. The plague of dusk expanded venomously and insidiously in all directions, creeping from one thing to another; whatever it touched at once decayed, blackened, and disintegrated into rot. People fled from the dusk in silent panic, but the leprosy soon caught up with them, smearing a dark rash across their foreheads. They lost their faces, which fell away in great, shapeless stains, and so they went on, without features, without eyes, dropping mask after mask along the way, until the dusk teemed with those abandoned larvae, scattered behind them. Everything was overgrown with black, rotting bark, which peeled away in great sheets and strips of darkness. And while down below everything was disintegrating and decaying in that quiet upheaval, in that panic of rapid decomposition, up above the silent alarm of the twilight rose higher and higher, quavering with the chatter of a million quiet little bells, swelling into a flight of a million invisible skylarks flying together into a great, silvery infinity. Then it was suddenly night—a vast night, swelling with the gusts of wind that expanded it. Into its many-pathed labyrinth, bright nests had been hewn: shops, like great coloured lanterns, filled with piles of goods and the hubbub of buyers. Through the bright windows of those lanterns, one could observe the loud and strangely ceremonial ritual of autumn shopping.

That immense, billowing autumn night—swollen with shadows and spread out by the winds—concealed bright pockets in its dark folds: sacks of colourful trinkets with a motley selection of chocolates, fruit cakes, and exotic colonial goods. Those kiosks and stalls— cobbled together from sweet boxes, papered with garish chocolate advertisements, filled with playful junk, soaps, gold-plated trifles, tinfoil, tubes, wafers, and coloured mints—were stations of light-heartedness, rattles of recklessness, scattered across the cliffs of the enormous, labyrinthine, wind-flapped night.

Great, glowering crowds flowed in the darkness, in noisy confusion, in the shuffle of a thousand feet, in the murmur of a thousand lips—a teeming, muddled migration proceeding along the arteries of the autumn town. And so that river flowed, filled with chatter, dark glances, wily scowls, fragmented conversations, finely-chopped tales—a great pulp of gossip, laughter, and commotion.

It seemed as if the surging crowds were made of dry, autumn poppy heads, spilling out their poppy seeds, or of rattle-heads and clapper-heads.

My father went about agitated and flushed, his eyes glistening in the brightly lit shop as he listened attentively.

Through the shop display windows and the entrance came the distant hum of the town, the muted chatter of the surging throng. Over the quiet of the shop, an oil lamp burned brightly, hanging from the high vaulting and dispelling the slightest trace of shadow from all the crannies and corners. The vast, empty floor cracked in the silence, counting out its glistening squares in the light—a chessboard of great tiles talking to one another in those loud cracks, answering here and there with a splitting sound. All the while, the rolls of cloth lay quietly in their felt fluffiness, without a sound, exchanging glances behind Father's back and sending conspiratorial signals from cabinet to cabinet.

Father listened. In the nocturnal silence, his ear seemed to grow and expand through the window into a fantastical coral, a red polyp waving in the currents of the night.

He listened and he heard. He heard with growing anxiety the distant tide of the approaching crowds. He glanced around the empty shop in terror. He searched for the shop assistants. But those dark- and red-haired angels had disappeared somewhere. He was left alone, fearful of the crowds that would soon flood the silence of the shop in a raucous, plundering horde to divide the spoils amongst themselves, auctioning off that whole rich autumn, gathered over so many years in that great, quiet granary.

Where were the shop assistants? Where were those handsome cherubs, who were supposed to defend the dark cloth ramparts? Father suspected with a painful intuition that they were off somewhere in our house sinning with other people's daughters. Standing motionless and filled with anxiety, eyes glistening in the bright silence of the shop, he sensed with his inner ear what was happening in the depths of the house, in the back chambers of that great, coloured lantern. The house opened up before him, room by room, chamber by chamber, like a house of cards, and he saw the shop assistants chasing after Adela through all those empty, brightly lit spaces, downstairs and upstairs, until she slipped away from them and burst into the bright kitchen, where she barricaded herself in with the kitchen sideboard.

There she stood, breathless, radiant, and amused, fluttering her long eyelashes with a smile. The shop assistants sniggered as they crouched behind the door. The kitchen window was open to the vast, black night, filled with hallucinations and tangled lines. The black windowpanes, slightly ajar, burned with the reflection of distant illuminations. Shiny pots and cylinders stood motionless all around, their oily glaze glistening in the silence. Adela cautiously leant her flushed, painted face out of the window, eyes aflutter. She looked for the shop assistants in the dark yard, certain they were lying in ambush. She spotted them as they crept in single file along the wall on a narrow cornice under a first-floor window, in the red glare of the distant illuminations, edging towards the kitchen window. Father bellowed in anger and despair, but at that moment the hubbub of voices came very near and the bright windows of the shop were suddenly populated by faces contorted with laughter, chattering faces that flattened their noses against the shiny windowpanes. Father went purple with outrage and leapt up onto the counter. When the crowd stormed the fortress, bursting into the shop in a raucous mob, my father scaled the shelves of cloth in a single bound and thus suspended high above the crowd blew with all his might into a great trombone made of horn to sound the alarm. Yet the vaulting did not fill with the flutter of angels hastening to his aid; instead every groan of the horn was answered by the great laughing choir of the crowd.

'Jakub, time to trade! Jakub, time to sell!' they all cried, and their cries, repeated over and over in unison, began to form a rhythm, slowly turning into the melody of a refrain sung by all their throats together.

My father admitted defeat, jumping down from his high cornice and rushing with a shout towards the barricades of cloth. Swollen with anger, his head bulging into a purple fist, he dashed, like a militant prophet, to the cloth ramparts and began to rage against them. He rammed his whole body into the heavy bales of wool, tipping them out of their places. He slipped himself under the enormous rolls of cloth, hoisted them onto his stooped shoulders, and then brought them down from the heights of the gallery onto the counter with a dull thud. As they flew through the air, the bales unfurled themselves with a flutter into enormous banners, while the shelves exploded on all sides with bursts of drapery and waterfalls of cloth, as if at the touch of Moses's staff.

And so the stock poured out of the cabinets, vomiting down and flowing into wide rivers. The colourful contents of the shelves surged, swelled, and multiplied, flooding all the counters and tables.

The walls of the shop disappeared under the imposing formations of that cloth cosmogony, under chains of mountains rising in mighty massifs. Wide valleys opened up between the mountain slopes, and the lines of continents glowered in the grand pathos of the highlands. The space of the shop expanded into the panorama of an autumn landscape, filled with lakes and distant prospects. Against the background of this scenery, my father wandered amidst the folds and valleys of a fantastical Canaan, walking in great strides with his hands spread wide into the clouds like a prophet, shaping paradise with the strokes of his inspiration.

Yet down below, at the foot of the Mount Sinai that had grown out of Father's anger, the people gesticulated, blasphemed, worshipped Baal, and traded. They scooped up whole armfuls of soft folds, draping themselves in colourful cloth, wrapping themselves in improvised domino cloaks and coats, chattering profusely and disjointedly.

Suddenly my father rose up above those gangs of pedlars, enormous with anger, and thundered from on high at the idolaters with a mighty word. Then, transported with despair, he clambered up onto the high galleries of cabinets and dashed headlong along the trusses of the shelves, along the rattling boards of the bare scaffolding, pursued by images of the shameless debauchery that he sensed behind his back in the depths of the house. The shop assistants had just reached the iron balcony at the level of the window, where they seized Adela around her waist to drag her out through the window, still fluttering her eyes and trailing her slender legs behind her in silk stockings.

As my father merged the fury of his gestures into the prose of the landscape, terrified by the abomination of sin, the reckless tribe of Baal down below surrendered themselves to lascivious merrymaking. A kind of parodic passion, a plague of laughter, overtook the rabble. For how could one demand seriousness from such a gang of rattlers and nutcrackers! How could one demand sympathy for Father's many cares from those grinders, ceaselessly grinding their colourful pulp of words! Deaf to the thunderbolts of prophetic anger, the traders crouched down in little throngs, dressed in silk bekishes, beside the wrinkled mountains of material, garrulously discussing the virtues of the goods amidst much laughter. Those black-market pedlars spread the noble substance of the landscape around on quick tongues, grinding it down with the chopping of their chatter and almost swallowing it.

Elsewhere, groups of Jews stood around in colourful gabardines and great fur kalpaks before high waterfalls of bright material. They were the elders of the Great Assembly, stately gentlemen filled with solemn dignity, stroking long, well-tended beards, and holding restrained, diplomatic conversations. But even in these ceremonial conversations, in the looks they exchanged, there was a gleam of winking irony. In between these groups, the common people came and went in a featureless crowd, a rabble without faces or individuality. They seemed to fill the gaps in the landscape, lining the background with the little bells and rattles of their mindless chatter. They were a clownish element, a dancing crowd of Punchinellos and harlequins, who—without any serious commercial intentions of their own—reduced the transactions being conducted here and there to absurdity with their clownish pranks.

Gradually growing bored with clowning, the merry little crowd dispersed into distant regions of the landscape, where they slowly lost themselves among the rocky niches and valleys. One by one, those jokers fell into the cracks and folds of the terrain, like children worn out from playing in the nooks and crannies of an apartment on the night of a ball.

Meanwhile, the fathers of the town, the elders of the Great Sanhedrin, strolled about in groups, filled with gravity and dignity, carrying on their quiet, profound disputations. Scattered over the entirety of that vast, mountainous country, they wandered in twos and threes on distant, winding roads. Their small, dark silhouettes populated the desert uplands under a dark, heavy sky, wrinkled and cloudy, ploughed into long, parallel furrows, into white and silver ridges, revealing further layers of stratification in its depths.

The light of the lamp created an artificial day in that country: a strange day without dawn or evening.

My father was slowly calming down. His anger settled and hardened into the layers and strata of the landscape. He sat upon the galleries of the high shelves and gazed out at that vast autumnal country. He saw people fishing in distant lakes. The fishermen sat in little coracles, two in each boat, casting their nets out into the water. On the banks, boys carried baskets on their heads, filled with the slapping, silvery catch.

Then he saw groups of wanderers in the distance raising their heads to the sky and pointing at something with outstretched hands.

Suddenly the sky was teeming with a kind of colourful rash; it broke out in rippling stains that spread, ripened, and soon filled the expanse with a strange species of birds, circling and wheeling in great, overlapping spirals. The whole sky was filled with their lofty flights, the flapping of their wings, the majestic lines of their quiet soaring. Some of them, like giant storks, floated motionless on calmly outstretched wings; others, like the colourful head-dresses or trophies of savages, flapped ponderously and clumsily just to stay aloft on waves of warm air; still others were but awkward conglomerations of wings, huge feet, and plucked necks, resembling poorly stuffed vultures or condors with the sawdust leaking out of them.

Among them were two-headed birds, many-winged birds, and crippled birds that floundered through the air in decrepit, single-winged flight. The sky began to resemble an old fresco, filled with freaks and fantastical creatures that wheeled past one another and returned in colourful ellipses.

My father lifted himself up on the trusses, bathed in a sudden glow, reached out his hands, and summoned the birds with an old incantation. Filled with emotion, he recognized them. They were the distant, long-forgotten progeny of that avian generation that Adela had driven away to all corners of the sky. Now they were returning, debased and exuberant: an artificial progeny, a degenerate avian tribe, wasted away inside.

They had shot up to a ridiculous size, absurdly enormous, while inside they were empty and lifeless. All the vitality of those birds had passed into their plumage, which was fantastically luxuriant. They were like a museum of extinct species, a junk room of avian Paradise.

Some of them flew upside down, with heavy, clumsy beaks like padlocks, overloaded with colourful growths. They were also blind. How this unexpected return moved my father! How he marvelled at their avian instinct, at the attachment to their Master that this exiled bloodline had nurtured as a legend in their souls, until finally, after many generations, on the last day before the extinction of their tribe, they had come home to their ancient fatherland.

Yet those blind paper birds no longer recognized Father. In vain, he called out to them in the old incantation, the forgotten tongue of birds; they could neither hear him nor see him.

Suddenly there were stones whistling through the air. It was those jokers, that stupid, mindless tribe, who had begun to hurl missiles into the fantastical avian sky.

In vain, my father warned them; in vain, he threatened them with imploring gestures. They would not hear him or pay him any mind. And so the birds fell. Struck by missiles, they sagged and withered in the air. By the time they hit the ground, they were nothing but a formless heap of feathers.

In the blink of an eye, the uplands were covered with that strange, fantastical carrion. Before my father could rush to the place of the slaughter, the whole magnificent tribe of birds lay dead, stretched out on the rocks.

Only now, from up close, could Father observe the misery of that impoverished generation, the ridiculousness of their trashy anatomy.

They were enormous clumps of feathers, stuffed shoddily like old carcasses. In many of them, it was impossible to tell the head apart, as that cudgelled part of the body bore no trace of soul. Some of them were covered with shaggy, matted fur, like a bison's, and reeked with a repulsive odour. Others resembled dead camels, hunchbacked and bald. Still others were clearly made of a kind of paper, empty inside, but beautifully coloured without. Some of them turned out from up close to be nothing other than large peacocks' tails, colourful fans into which a semblance of life had been breathed in some incomprehensible way.

I watched my father's sad return. The artificial day slowly took on the colours of an ordinary morning. In the ravaged shop, the highest shelves savoured the bright hues of the morning sky. Among the fragments of the faded landscape, among the demolished stage set of the scenes of the night, my father found the shop assistants waking from their slumber. They got up among bales of cloth, yawning at the sun. In the kitchen upstairs, Adela, still warm from sleep and with hair dishevelled, was grinding coffee in the mill, pressing it against her white bosom, which imparted a glow of heat to the beans. The cat cleaned itself in the sunshine.

THE BOOK

I CALL IT SIMPLY the Book, without qualifiers or epithets, and there is in this abstinence and restraint a kind of helpless sigh, a quiet capitulation before the greatness of the transcendent. For no word or allusion could possibly shine, smell, or tremble with that shiver of terror, that presentiment of a thing without a name, the first aftertaste of which on the tip of our tongue surpasses our capacity for wonder. What good would the pathos of adjectives and the fuzziness of epithets do in the face of that thing beyond measure, that splendour beyond any accounting? After all, the reader, the true reader on whom this tale depends, will understand, as I look him straight in the eye, glowing from deep inside with that brilliant light. In that short, strong look, in a fleeting squeeze of the hand, he will grasp, comprehend, and accept everything, closing his eyes in rapture at this profound reception. For under the table between us aren't we all secretly holding hands?

The Book . . . Somewhere in earliest childhood, at the first dawn of life, the horizon glowed with its gentle light. It lay in all its glory on Father's desk, while my father, silently immersed in it, patiently rubbed the spine of those decals with a moistened finger until the blank paper began to fog up and become cloudy with blissful anticipation, suddenly shedding scraps of blotting paper to reveal a peacock's eye margin framed with lashes, as my own eyes dropped, half-closing, to a virgin dawn of divine colours, to the wondrous wetness of the purest azures.

O, that wiping away of the scales; o, that invasion of radiance; o, blissful spring; o, Father . . .

Sometimes Father would rise from the Book and leave the room. Then I was left alone with it, as the wind blew through its pages and the images leapt up.

And while the wind quietly leafed through the sheets, blowing out colours and shapes, a shiver ran through the columns of its text, releasing flights of swallows and larks from between the letters. It soared, scattering page after page and melting into the landscape, which it saturated with its colours. Sometimes it slept, the wind fanning it quietly like a hundred-leafed rose, as it opened its leaves, petal by petal, eyelid after eyelid—all of them blind, velvety, and drowsy, concealing an azure pupil in their depths, a peacock's core, a screaming nest of hummingbirds.

That was long ago. My mother did not yet exist for me. I spent the days alone with my father in our room, then as vast as the world.

Prismatic crystals, hanging from the lamp, filled the room with refracted colours that scattered in a rainbow to all corners; as the lamp twisted on its chain, the whole room shifted with those fragments of colour, as if the spheres of the seven planets were spinning past one another. I liked to stand between Father's legs, hugging them on both sides like pillars. Sometimes he wrote letters. I would sit at the desk and follow with wonder the flourishes of his signature, swirling and elaborate, like the trills of a coloratura singer. In the wallpaper, smiles budded, eyes hatched, and pranks turned somersaults. To entertain me, Father blew soap bubbles into that rainbow space through a long straw. They bounced off the walls and burst, leaving their colours behind them in the air.

Then my mother arrived, and that bright early idyll came to an end. Seduced by Mother's caresses, I forgot about Father; my life moved off along a new and different track, without holidays and miracles, and I would have forgotten about the Book forever if not for that night and that dream.

2.

Once I awoke on a dark winter's morning, the gloomy dawn glowing from under piles of darkness, with foggy forms and signs still swimming beneath my eyelids, and I began to rave in anguish and helpless sorrow about the old lost Book.

Nobody could understand what I wanted. Irritated by their obtuseness, I began to badger and pester my parents with feverish impatience.

Barefoot and dressed in only a shirt, trembling with excitement, I rummaged through my father's library, disappointed and angry, trying desperately to describe to my dumbfounded audience that indescribable thing, which no word or image traced by my trembling finger could ever equal. I exhausted myself in explanations filled with tangled contradictions, and then wept in impotent despair.

They stood above me, helpless and confused, ashamed of their powerlessness. Deep in their hearts, they knew they were not without blame. My rage—the impatient and furious tone of my demands—gave me the appearance of being in the right, the superiority of a well-founded complaint. They came running with various books and thrust them into my hands. I threw them down with indignation.

One of them, a hefty folio, my father kept trying to pass to me with timid encouragement. I opened it. It was the Bible. On its pages, I saw a great migration of animals pouring down the roads and branching out in columns across a vast country; I saw the sky covered in fluttering flocks of birds—an enormous, inverted pyramid whose distant apex touched the Ark.

I looked up at Father, my eyes filled with accusation: 'You know!' I cried. 'You know perfectly well! Don't pretend! Don't try to weasel out of it! This book has given you away. Why do you hand me these tainted apocrypha, this thousandth copy of a copy, this shoddy falsification? What have you done with the Book?'

Father averted his eyes.

3.

Weeks passed and my agitation subsided, but the image of the Book still burned in my soul with a bright flame—a great, rustling Codex, a ruffled Bible through whose pages the wind blew, plundering it like an enormous, disintegrating rose.

My father, seeing that I had calmed down, approached me cautiously and said in a tone of mild suggestion: 'In reality, there are only books. *The* Book is a myth we believe in when we're young, but then we stop taking it seriously as the years go by.' I had already formed a different view. I knew that the Book was a demand, a task. I felt the burden of a great mission upon my shoulders. I said nothing in reply, filled with contempt and a fierce, grim pride.

For at that time I was already in possession of those scraps of a book, those pathetic remnants, which in a strange stroke of fortune had slipped into my hands. I carefully hid the treasure away from prying eyes, mourning the downfall of a book whose mutilated remains would win nobody's sympathy. This is how it happened.

One winter's day, I had come across Adela, with brush in hand, leaning on the writing desk, where a sheaf of tattered papers lay. I leant over her shoulder, not so much from curiosity as to intoxicate myself with the scent of her body, whose youthful charms had revealed themselves to my recently awakened senses.

'Look,' she said, tolerating my embrace without protest. 'Is it possible for someone's hair to grow right down to the ground? I'd like to have hair like that.'

I looked at the illustration. On a large folio page was an image of a woman with a sturdy, dumpy figure and a face filled with vigour and experience. From the head of that lady flowed an enormous sheepskin of hair, tumbling voluminously down her back, its ends sweeping the ground in thick plaits. It was the most improbable prank of nature: a vast, billowing cloak hitched to the roots of her hair. It was difficult to imagine that the weight of it did not cause her severe pain or even incapacitate the head that supported it. But the owner of this splendour seemed to carry it with pride, and the accompanying text told the story of the miracle in bold print, beginning with the words: *I, Anna Csillag, born in Karlovice in Moravia, had a meagre growth of hair . . .*

It was a lengthy tale, similar in structure to the story of Job. Anna Csillag had been afflicted with a meagre growth of hair in an act of divine retribution. The whole town pitied her for this impairment, which they forgave in view of her immaculate life—though she could not have been entirely blameless. And so it transpired that their vehement prayers caused the curse to be lifted from her head. Anna Csillag was granted the grace of enlightenment. She received signs and instructions to concoct a preparation, a miraculous medicine that would restore her head's fertility. Her hair began to sprout, and that was not all. Her husband, brothers, and cousins were soon covered with a heavy, black fur of stubble. On the opposite page, Anna Csillag was depicted six weeks after the revelation of her recipe, surrounded by brothers, brothers-in-law, nephews, and moustachioed elders with beards hanging down to their belts. We stared with admiration at that veritable explosion of unfeigned, bearish masculinity. Anna Csillag brought joy to the whole town, on which a true benediction had descended in the form of those great wavy shocks and manes of hair, its inhabitants now sweeping the ground with their beards like thick brooms. Anna Csillag became the apostle of hairiness. After bringing joy to her native town, she wished to take it to the whole world, and so she asked, begged, and cajoled them all to accept this gift from God for their salvation, this miraculous medicine of which she alone knew the secret.

I read the story over Adela's shoulder, and then suddenly I was struck by a thought whose touch left me all in flames. Why, this was the Book—its last pages, its unauthorized appendix, a back annexe filled with scraps and junk! The fragments of the rainbow revolved on the whirling wallpaper. I tore the pages from Adela's hands, and blurted out in a voice that I could not control: 'Where did you get this book?'

'Stupid boy,' she replied, shrugging her shoulders. 'It has always been here; every day we tear pages from it to wrap the meat from the butcher's and your father's breakfast.'

4.

I ran to my room. Shaken to the core, my face burning, I began to flip through the tattered pages with trembling hands. To my disappointment, there were barely a dozen of them. Not a single page of the text itself—just advertisements and announcements. After the prophecies of the long-haired sibyl came a page devoted to a wondrous medicine for curing all manner of illnesses and ailments. Elsa—the fluid with the swan—was the name of that miracle-working balm. The page was filled with the moving accounts and testimonies of people who had experienced its wonders.

The convalescents came from Transylvania, from Slavonia, from Bucovina, filled with enthusiasm to testify, to tell their stories in ardent, emotive words. They came bandaged and stooped, shaking their now superfluous crutches, throwing off the plasters from their eyes and the bands from their scrofula sores.

In the wanderings of these cripples, one saw sad, faraway little towns under skies as white as paper, hardened with the prose of everyday life. These were towns that had been forgotten in the very depths of time, where people were bound to their little fates, which they could not escape even for a moment. A cobbler was a cobbler through and through: he smelt of leather; his face was small and emaciated, with pale, short-sighted eyes over a drab, sniffling moustache; he felt like a cobbler to his marrow. And if their ulcers did not hurt, if their bones did not break, and if dropsy did not confine them to their rough beds, then they were happy with a drab, grey happiness. They smoked cheap tobacco, yellow imperial-royal tobacco, or daydreamed vacantly in front of the lottery office. Cats scampered across the road in front of them from left and right; they dreamt of black dogs and their hands itched. Sometimes they wrote letters on sheets of letter paper, carefully sticking on the stamps and distrustfully confiding them to the postbox, which they struck with a fist as if to wake it up. White doves then flew through their dreams with letters in their beaks, vanishing into the clouds.

The next pages rose above the sphere of everyday affairs into regions of pure poetry.

There were concertinas, zithers, and harps—the ancient instruments of angelic choirs, available now, thanks to the progress of industry, at prices affordable to the common man, the god-fearing folk, for the warming of hearts and wholesome entertainment.

There were barrel organs, those veritable wonders of technology—filled with hidden flutes, throats, pipes, mouth organs trilling sweetly like nests of sobbing nightingales—a priceless treasure for invalids, a source of lucrative earnings for cripples, and generally indispensable in every musical home. One saw those beautifully painted barrel organs wandering along on the backs of grey, inconspicuous old men, whose faces, emaciated by life, seemed to be covered in cobwebs, entirely indistinct: faces with teary, motionless eyes that were slowly disappearing; faces emptied of life, drained of colour and innocent, like the bark of a tree cracked by all manner of weather, smelling only of rain and sky.

They had long since forgotten their own names and who they were, so they shuffled confusedly along in their heavy shoes, with their crooked knees, taking small, even steps in monotonously straight lines amidst the twisted, convoluted paths of passers-by.

On white, sunless afternoons stale with winter, immersed in the everyday affairs of the day, they would unobtrusively extricate themselves from the crowd and set up their barrel organ on a stand at a street corner, under a yellow streak of sky dissected by a telegraph wire, among the people hurrying vacantly along with collars upturned. They would begin their melody, not from the beginning, but from where they had left off yesterday, playing 'Daisy, Daisy, give me your answer do . . .' as white plumes of steam puffed out of the chimneys. Strangely, that melody, only just begun, slipped at once into an empty slot, into its allotted place at that hour and in that landscape, as if it had always belonged to that day, pensive and lost in itself, while the thoughts and grey cares of the hastening passers-by merged with its rhythm.

And when, after a certain time, the melody ended—in a long-drawn-out shriek expelled from the entrails of the organ as it started up a new tune—those thoughts and cares stopped for a moment, as if to change their step in the dance, and then without a moment's hesitation began to spin again in the oppo-site direction, to the beat of the new melody flowing from the pipes of the barrel organ: 'Małgorzata, treas-ure of my soul . . .'

And in the dull indifference of that afternoon, nobody even noticed that the meaning of the world had changed entirely, no longer running to the beat of 'Daisy, Daisy,' but, on the contrary, to 'Mał-go-rzata . . .'

We turn the next page . . . Now what? Is the spring rain falling? No, it's the chirping of little birds, sprinkling down like grey pellets on an umbrella—for here they offer up the finest canaries, cages filled with goldfishes and starlings, baskets filled with songbirds and winged natterers. Light and spindle-like, as if stuffed with cotton wool, leaping with a flutter, as if on smooth, warbling pivots, twittering like cuckoo clocks, they were a comfort to the lonely, a substitute for the family hearth for bachelors, extracting from even the hardest of hearts a warmth of maternal feeling, so tiny and touching were they, and when one turned the page above them, they sent off the departing reader with an enchanting chorus of twittering.

But still that doleful script tumbled down into an ever deeper decline. Now it descended into the trackless wilderness of a dubious, charlatan soothsaying. For who was this gentleman in his long cloak, with a smile half-devoured by a black beard, offering his services to the public? It was Signor Bosco of Milan, a self-styled master of black magic, who spoke indistinctly and at great length, demonstrating something on his fingertips without making the thing any more comprehensible. And although in his own opinion he was reaching astonishing conclusions, which he seemed to weigh between his delicate fingers before their volatile meanings escaped into the air, and although he emphasized the subtle hinges of his dialectics with a cautionary raising of his eyebrows, preparing the audience for extraordinary things, one always failed to comprehend him. Even worse, one had no wish to comprehend, leaving him with his gesticulations, his hushed tones, and the whole gamut of his dark smiles, so as to flip through the last, disintegrating pages.

On these final pages, which had evidently descended into hallucinatory ravings and flagrant absurdity, a gentleman was offering up a foolproof method for becoming energetic and decisive, droning on and on about principles and character. And yet it was enough to turn the page again to become entirely disoriented in any matters of decisiveness or principle.

There, in mincing steps constricted by the train of her dress, came a certain Madame Magda Wang, who declared from the lofty heights of her plunging décolletage that she laughed in the face of male decisiveness and principles, and that her speciality was precisely to break even the strongest of characters. (Here, with a movement of her leg, she rearranged the train on the ground.) For this purpose, there are methods, she continued between clenched teeth, foolproof methods that she did not wish to discuss here, referring readers instead to her memoirs, entitled *Purple Days* (The Anthroposophical Institute Press in Budapest), in which she had chronicled her colonial experiences in the field of man-taming (she uttered this phrase with emphasis and an ironic flash of her eyes). Strangely, this lady, whose words were so brusque and dismissive, seemed certain of the approval of those of whom she spoke with such cynicism; amidst a peculiar vertigo and flickering of the light, one felt that the directions of moral orientation had somehow shifted, and that we were now in a very different climate in which the compass of feelings worked in reverse.

This was the final word of the Book, which left an aftertaste of strange bewilderment, a mixture of hunger and arousal in the soul.

5.

Bent over the Book, my face burning like a rainbow, I quietly smouldered from ecstasy to ecstasy. Immersed in reading, I forgot about dinner. My intuition had not been mistaken. This was the Authentic, the sacred original—though sunk in profound indignity and degradation. And when in the late dusk, smiling bliss-fully, I put those scraps of paper away in the deepest drawer of the chest, hiding them behind other books, it seemed to me that I was putting the twilight to bed—a twilight that kept rekindling itself, passing through all the flames and purples, and then returning again, not wanting to end.

How indifferent I became to all other books!

For ordinary books are like meteors. Each of them has its moment, an instant in which it ascends with a scream like a phoenix, all its pages burning. In that one moment, for that one instant, we love them, though even then they are already but ashes. With bitter resignation, we sometimes wander in the late hours through those cool pages, shifting their dead phrases, like rosary beads, with a wooden rattle.

The exegetes of the Book claim that all books aspire to the Authentic. They live a borrowed life, returning in the moment of their ascension to their ancient source. This means that books dwindle away, while the Authentic grows. Yet we do not wish to weary the reader with a lecture on the Doctrine. We would merely like to turn his attention to one thing: that the Authentic lives and grows. What does this mean? That next time we open our sheaf of scraps, who knows where Anna Csillag and her followers will be. Maybe we will see her, a long-haired pilgrim sweeping the roads of Moravia with her cloak, wandering through a distant country, through white cities immersed in everyday prose, handing out samples of Elsa fluid balm to God's simpletons, plagued with pus and scabies. What then will the good-natured, bearded elders of the little town do, immobilized by their enormous growths? And what then will the faithful crowd do, condemned to the cultivation and administration of their inflated harvests? Who knows if they won't all purchase original Black Forest barrel organs and set off into the world to find their hirsute apostle, seeking her throughout the land, playing 'Daisy, Daisy' wherever they go?

O, odyssey of bearded ones, wandering with those barrel organs from town to town in search of their spiritual mother! When will a rhapsody worthy of that epic be found? But in whose hands have they now left the town that was confided to their care? To whom have they entrusted the hearts and minds of the city of Anna Csillag? Could they not have foreseen that—deprived of its spiritual elite, of its splendid patriarchs—the town would soon fall into doubt and apostasy, opening its gates—to whom?—ah, to the cynical and perverse Magda Wang (The Anthroposophical Institute Press in Budapest), who would found a school for the taming and breaking of characters there?

But let us return to our pilgrims.

For who among us does not recognize that old guard, those wandering Cimbri, with their dark black hair and seemingly powerful bodies made from tissue without any real vigour or juices? Their whole strength and might have gone into their hair. Anthropologists have been wracking their brains for many a year over that curious race, always dressed in black, with heavy silver chains on their bellies and thick brass signet rings on their fingers.

I like them, those interchangeable Caspars and Balthazars, with their profound gravity, their funereal decorativeness, those splendid manly specimens with beautiful eyes filled with the oily gleam of roasted coffee. I like the noble lack of vitality in their bulging, spongy bodies, the morbidezza of expiring families, the panting breath from powerful chests, and even the smell of valerian that their beards exude.

Like Angels of the Presence, they sometimes stand unexpectedly at the doors to our kitchens, enormous and panting, easily exhausted. They wipe the sweat from clammy foreheads, rolling the blue whites of their eyes, suddenly forgetting their mission, searching in bemusement for an excuse, a pretext for their coming, until finally they reach out their hands for alms.

We return to the Authentic. Of course we never left it. But now we point to a strange quality of those tattered Scraps, no doubt already obvious to the reader: that they unravel as we read them, that their borders are open on all sides to flows and fluctuations.

Now, for instance, nobody offers goldfinches, for those feather dusters have been fluttering out at irregular intervals from the barrel organs of the dark-haired gentlemen, from among the breaks and folds in the melodies, and the market square is now covered with them, as if with a colourful typeface. Ah, what a flickering proliferation, filled with twittering ... Around all the spikes, poles, and weathervanes they form a veritable traffic jam of colour, fluttering and fighting for space. It's enough to stick a rod out the window for a few moments to haul it back into the room covered with a heavy, flapping swarm.

In our story, we are now approaching with rapid steps that splendid, catastrophic age that in our biography bears the name of the age of genius.

It would be in vain to deny that we feel a certain pounding of the heart, a blessed anxiety, the sacred nervousness that precedes final things. Soon we will run out of colours in the crucibles, and of brightness in the soul, both of which we require to lay down the highest notes, to sketch out the most luminous and transcendent outlines of this painting.

What is the age of genius and when was it?

Here we are forced to become entirely esoteric for a moment, like Signor Bosco of Milan, lowering our voices to a hoarse whisper. We punctuate our arguments with ambiguous smiles and rub the delicate material of imponderables between our fingertips like a pinch of salt. It is not our fault if we sometimes take on the air of those vendors of invisible fabrics, displaying their fraudulent wares with elaborate gestures.

So did the age of genius happen or did it not happen? It is hard to say. Both yes and no. For there are things that can never happen completely. They are too great and splendid to fit into a single event. They can only try to happen, testing whether the ground of reality will hold their weight.

Then they withdraw, afraid to lose their integrity in the imperfection of their execution. But if they have chipped away at their capital, losing one thing or another in these attempts at incarnation, they soon jealously gather up their property again, calling it back and reintegrating themselves. Those white stains remain in our biography: fragrant stigmata, silvery traces of bare angelic feet scattered in enormous steps through our days and nights, while the fullness of glory grows and increases, culminating above us and passing triumphantly from rapture to rapture.

And yet in a certain sense it fits, whole and integral, into every one of its imperfect and fragmentary incarnations. Here the phenomenon of representation or surrogate being comes into play. A given event may be small and impoverished in its provenance and resources, and yet, when held up close to the eye, it opens in its depths an infinite and radiant perspective as a higher order of being strives to express itself, shining fiercely from within it.

And so we shall gather up all the allusions, the earthly approximations, the stations and stages on the roads of our life, like the fragments of a broken mirror. Piece by piece, we shall gather up that which is one and indivisible: our great age, the age of genius of our life.

Perhaps in our diminished aspirations, terrorized by the indifference of the transcendent, we have needlessly restricted ourselves, doubting and wavering. When in spite of all our reservations: it existed.

It existed, and nothing can take that certainty away from us, that luminous flavour we can still taste on our tongues, that cold fire on the palate, that sigh as wide as the sky and fresh as a gulp of pure ultramarine.

Have we prepared the reader to some degree for the things to come? Can we now risk a journey into the age of genius? Our nerves have infected the reader. We can sense his anxiety. In spite of the appearance of excitement, our heart is heavy and we are filled with fear. In the name of God, then, all aboard and off we go!

THE AGE OF GENIUS

I.

ORDINARY FACTS ARE arranged in time, strung out on its sequence like a thread. There they have their antecedents and their consequences, which bunch up together, following hard on each other's heels without gaps or interruptions. This also has its implications for narrative, the soul of which is continuity and succession.

But what to do with those events that do not have their own place in time, with events that come too late, when all of time has already been distributed, divided, snapped up, and so now they are left out in the cold—unclassified, suspended in mid-air, lost and homeless?

Could it be that time is too narrow for all events? Can it happen that all the seats of time have already been sold? We jog anxiously down the whole train of events as it prepares to depart.

For the love of God, surely there's a black market here somewhere on tickets for time? . . . Please, Mr Conductor!

Calm down! We can sort it all out quietly amongst ourselves, without any needless panic.

Has the reader ever heard of parallel streams in double-track time? Yes, there are side branches of time, admittedly illegal and dubious, but when one is transporting contraband, as we are—a supernumerary, unclassified event—then one can't be too fussy. So let us try to shoot off a side branch at some point in the story, a blind track, and then shunt the illegal events onto it. Have no fear. It will all happen imperceptibly; the reader won't experience any disturbance. Who knows—perhaps, even as we speak, this underhanded manipulation is already behind us, and we are rolling down that blind track.

2.

My mother dashed in, terrified, and enfolded my scream in her arms, trying to smother it like a fire, putting it out in the folds of her love. She closed my mouth with her own mouth and began to scream together with me.

But I pushed her away and pointed at the fiery pillar, the golden beam that hung diagonally in the air like a splinter that would not be removed, filled with radiant light and dust circulating within it. I screamed: 'Tear it out, rip it out!'

The stove puffed up with the great colourful daub painted on its forehead, flushed with blood, and it seemed that the convulsions of those veins and sinews, the whole anatomy swollen to bursting point, had let out the raucous screech of a cockerel.

I stood with arms spread, inspired, pointing with outstretched fingers, pointing in anger, with stern concentration, taut as a signpost and trembling with ecstasy.

My hand led me, pale and alien, dragging me along: a stiffened, waxen appendage, like a great votive hand, like an angelic hand raised in an oath.

It was towards the end of winter. The days stood in puddles and embers, their palates filled with fire and pepper. Gleaming knives cut the honeyed pulp of the day into silver slices, into prisms filled with a spectrum of colours and piquant spices. The clock face of noon gathered the whole splendour of those days into a narrow space, displaying all the hours as they glowed with fire.

At that hour, unable to contain the heat, the day shed sheets of silver metal and crunching tinfoil, layer by layer, revealing its core of pure radiance. And as if that were not enough, the chimneys smoked, belching out a shimmering steam, while each moment burst with a flight of angels, a storm of wings devoured by the hungry sky, ever open to new explosions. Its bright battlements exploded with white plumes, its distant fortalices unfolding into quiet fans of accumulated explosions under the gleaming cannonade of invisible artillery.

The window of the room, already filled to the brim with sky, expanded with those endless flights, spilling out over the sheer curtains, which—all in flames and smoking in the fire—rippled with golden shadows and quivering rings of air. On the rug lay that slanted, glowing quadrilateral, shimmering with light. I could not tear myself away from it. That fiery pillar shook me to my core. I stood bewitched, legs astride, barking out harsh, alien imprecations at it in a changed voice.

On the threshold, in the entrance hall, they all stood wringing their hands in terrified consternation: relatives, neighbours, aunties in their Sunday best. They approached on tiptoe and then retreated, peering through the doorway, filled with curiosity. And I kept screaming.

'You see!' I screamed at my mother and brother. 'I always told you that everything was dammed up, walled in with boredom, unliberated. And now just look at this outpouring, at this blooming of everything, at this bliss!'

I wept with happiness and helplessness.

'Wake up!' I cried. 'Help me! Hurry! Can I handle this deluge alone? Can I stop the flood? How am I alone to answer the million dazzling questions with which God is inundating me?'

And when they remained silent I cried out in anger: 'Make haste! Fill your buckets with this abundance! Gather up your stores!'

But nobody would come to my aid. They all stood there helplessly, looking around and retreating behind their neighbours.

Then I understood what I had to do. Filled with fervour, I began to clear the cabinets of old folio volumes—Father's disintegrating account books, covered with his handwriting—and threw them onto the floor under the fiery pillar as it shone in the air. I couldn't find enough paper. My mother and brother kept running in with fresh armfuls of old newspapers, hurling them onto the pile on the ground. I sat among those papers, blinded by the glow, eyes filled with explosions, rockets, and colours, and began to draw. I drew in a hurry, in a panic, crosswise, aslant, over pages of printed and handwritten words. Inspired, my coloured pencils flew through columns of illegible text, racing in brilliant scribbles, in reckless zigzags, which suddenly tapered into anagrams of visions, into rebuses of luminous revelations, before unravelling again into empty, blind bolts of lightning, searching for the trail of inspiration.

O, those luminous drawings, emerging as if from under the hand of another! O, those transparent colours and shades! How often I still find them in my dreams—even today, after so many years—at the bottom of old drawers, fresh and bright as the morning, still moist with the first dew of the day: figures, landscapes, faces!

O, those azures, freezing the breath with choking fear; o, those greens, greener than astonishment; o, those preludes and twitterings of colour, only barely intuited and striving to be named!

So why did I squander them back then with such reckless abandon in the frivolity of excess? I allowed our neighbours to ransack and plunder those piles of drawings. They collected whole folders of them, which wended their way to goodness knows how many homes and trash heaps. Adela wallpapered the kitchen with them, making it bright and colourful, as if snow had fallen overnight outside the window.

It was a style of drawing filled with cruelty, snares, and ambushes. I sat there, taut as a bow, motionless, lying in wait, while the papers burned brightly around me in the sunlight. Pinned down by my pencil, it was enough for one of those drawings to make the slightest movement to escape. Then my hand, trembling with new reflexes and impulses, would hurl itself ferociously at the drawing like a cat. Suddenly alien, predatory, and wild, it took bites at lightning speed out of the freak trying to flee from under my pencil. Only then did it loosen its grip on the paper, whose still, dead body unfurled its colourful, fantastical anatomy in my exercise book as if in an herbarium.

It was a murderous hunt, a life-or-death struggle. For who could distinguish the attacker from the attacked in that ball of snorting fury, in that tangle filled with squeals and terror! It sometimes happened that my hand leapt forward two or three times, only to catch its victim on the fourth or fifth sheet. More than once, my hand screamed out in pain in the pincers and claws of those monsters, as they writhed under the touch of my scalpel.

From one hour to the next, the visions gathered in ever greater crowds, flocking in, forming traffic jams, until one day all the highways and byways were teeming and flowing with processions, and the whole country branched out in great migrations that dispersed into long parades—endless pilgrimages of wild beasts and animals.

As if in Noah's day, those colourful processions flowed on in rivers of fur and manes, rippling backs and tails, heads nodding ceaselessly to the rhythm of their steps.

My room was the border and tollbooth. Here they stopped and crowded together, bleating beseechingly. They spun in circles, stamping fearfully and wildly on the spot—hunchbacked, horned beings, sewn into all the costumes and armours of zoology. Terrified by one another and alarmed by their own masquerade, they stared out with frightened, astonished eyes through the openings in their hairy hides, mooing plaintively as if gagged beneath their masks.

Were they waiting for me to name them, to solve the riddle that they could not comprehend? Were they asking me for their names, so as to enter into them and fill them with their being? Strange and hideous monsters came in—question creatures, proposal creatures—and I was forced to shout and shoo them off.

They backed away, lowering their heads and staring up from under their brows; soon they became lost in themselves and turned back, dissolving into nameless chaos, into a junk room of forms. How many backs, flat or hunched, passed under my hand! How many heads slipped under it with a velvety caress!

I understood then why animals have horns. It was the incomprehensible thing that their life could not contain—a wild, persistent caprice, a blind and mindless obstinacy. An *idée fixe*, grown out beyond the boundaries of their being, high above their head, suddenly emerging into the light and freezing into hard, tangible material. There it took on a wild shape, unpredictable and incredible, twisted into a fantastical, terrifying arabesque unseen by their own eyes, into an unknown cipher under the threat of which they lived. I understood now why those animals were so susceptible to wild, mindless panics and frightened frenzies: sucked into their own madness, they were unable to extricate themselves from the tangle of their horns; they looked out sadly between them, with lowered heads, as if trying to find a way out between their branches. Those horned animals were far from emancipation, carrying the stigma of their error on their heads with sadness and resignation.

Yet even further from the light were the cats. Their perfection was appalling. Locked in the precision and exactitude of their bodies, they knew neither error nor deviation. For a moment, they descended into the depths, to the very bottom of their being, and there they froze in soft fur, suddenly serious with a menacing solemnity, while their eyes became round like moons, absorbed into fiery craters. But a moment later, thrown up on the shore, to the surface, they yawned out their nothingness, disappointed and disillusioned.

In their life, filled with self-contained grace, there was no room for any choice. Bored in that prison of perfection, with no hope of escape, consumed by spleen, they moaned with furrowed lips, filled with pointless cruelty, in short, striped faces. Down below, martens, polecats, and foxes crept stealthily past—the thieves among animals, creatures of bad conscience. They seized their places in being by deceit, intrigue, and trickery, against the plan of creation, pursued by hatred, threatened, constantly on their guard, constantly in fear for their places—they fiercely loved their stolen existence, hiding away in their burrows, ready to be torn to pieces in defence of it.

Eventually, they had all passed through and silence descended on my room. Once again I began to draw, immersed in my scraps of paper, which breathed out light. The window was open; turtle doves trembled in the spring air on the ledge. Tilting their heads, they displayed their round, glassy eyes in profile, flighty and frightened. The days became soft at their ends, opalescent and luminous, then pearly and filled with a misty sweetness.

The Easter holidays arrived and my parents departed for the week to visit my married sister. I was left alone in the flat at the mercy of my inspirations. Adela brought me lunch and breakfast every day. I didn't notice her presence when she stopped on the threshold, dressed in her holiday best, exuding the scent of spring from all her tulles and foulards.

A mild breeze blew in through the open window, filling the room with the reflections of distant landscapes. For a moment, the wafted colours of the bright distances were suspended in the air; then they dispersed and dissipated into the azure shade, into tenderness and emotion. The flood of images subsided; the outpouring of visions abated and fell silent.

I was seated on the ground. Around me lay crayons and trays of paints, divine colours, azures exhaling freshness, greens straying to the very brink of astonishment. When I picked up a red crayon, fanfares of joyful redness burst into the bright world, all the balconies rippled with waves of red banners, and the houses lined up down the street in a triumphal row. Processions of municipal firemen in raspberry uniforms paraded along bright, happy roads, while gentlemen tipped cherry-coloured bowler hats. A cherry sweetness and a cherry twittering of goldfinches filled the air, infused with lavender and a gentle light.

As I reached for an azure colour, the gleam of a cobalt spring marched down the streets through all the windows, which opened, one after another, their panes jangling, filled with the same azure and with blue fire. The sheer curtains rose in alarm, and a light, joyful draught blew down the row through billowing muslins and oleanders on empty balconies, as if at the other end of that long, bright avenue somebody had appeared in the far distance and was approaching—radiant, preceded by the news of his coming, by a premonition, announced by flocks of swallows, by luminous heralds scattered from mile to mile.

3.

During the Easter holidays, in late March or early April, Tobiasz's son Szloma was always released from prison, having been locked up for the winter after the rows and uproars of the summer and autumn. One afternoon that spring, I spotted him through the window as he emerged from the hairdresser's shop, which served as the town barber and surgeon rolled into one. Szloma opened the gleaming glass door with a gentility acquired from prison discipline and skipped down the three wooden steps, refreshed and rejuvenated, his hair neatly cropped, dressed in a short frock coat and chequered trousers hitched up high, slim and youthful in spite of his forty years.

At that hour, Holy Trinity Square was empty and clean. After the spring thaw and mud, the pavement had been washed by heavy rains and dried out over many days of mild, discreet weather in vast days that were perhaps too expansive for so early in the season, drawn out beyond their measure, especially in the evenings, when the dusk was endlessly prolonged, still empty at its core, futile and barren in its immense expectation.

When Szloma shut the door to the hairdresser's behind him, the sky immediately entered its glass pane, as it had all the little windows up and down the building, which lay open to the pure depths of the shaded horizon.

After descending the steps, he found himself completely alone on the shore of the great, empty shell of the square, which rippled with the azure of a sunless sky.

The vast, clean square lay there that afternoon like a glass ball, like a new year as yet unbegun. Szloma stood on its shore, grey and subdued, overwhelmed by azures, not daring to shatter that perfect ball of the untouched day with any decision.

Only once a year, on the day of his release from prison, did Szloma feel so pure, unencumbered, and new. The day took him into itself, washed clean of sin, renewed, reconciled with the world, which opened with a sigh before him the pure circles of its horizons, crowned with quiet beauty.

He was in no hurry. He stood on the edge of the day, not daring to cross over or transgress with his dainty, youthful, slightly limping step into the gently vaulted conch of the afternoon.

A transparent shadow hung over the town. The silence of that third hour of the afternoon extruded the pure whiteness of chalk from the houses and noise-lessly dealt it out, like a deck of cards, around the square. After one round, it began again, drawing on reserves of white from the great baroque façade of the Holy Trinity Church, which hastily arranged its great ruffled robe like the immense shirt of God fluttering down from the heavens, folded into pilasters, avant-corps, and casings, unfurled in a pathos of volutes and archivolts.

Szloma lifted his face and sniffed the air. A light breeze carried the scent of oleanders, the scent of festive apartments and cinnamon. He sneezed violently with his famously explosive sneeze, causing the pigeons on the police guard house to start and fly away in terror. Szloma smiled to himself: God had given him a signal through the shock of his nostrils that spring had begun. It was a sign surer than the arrival of storks, and from then on the days would be punctuated by these detonations, which—lost in the hum of the town, sometimes close by and sometimes further off—glossed the event with their witty commentary.

'Szloma!' I called out from the window of our lower floor.

Szloma saw me, smiled his friendly smile, and saluted.

'We're the only ones on the whole square, me and you,' I said softly, as the swollen glass ball of the sky resonated like a barrel.

'Me and you,' he repeated with a sad smile. 'How empty the world is today.'

'We could divide it between ourselves and give it a new name—that's how open, unoccupied, and defenceless it is. On days like this, the Messiah comes to the very edge of the horizon and looks down on the earth. When he sees it so quiet and white, with its azures and its air of reflection, it can happen that he loses sight of the border, that the blueish ranges of the clouds open up into a passage, and that before he knows it he is descending to earth. And the earth, lost in its own thoughts, won't even notice who has descended onto its paths, and people will awake from their afternoon naps and not remember anything. The whole of history will be erased, and it will be like primeval times before history began.'

'Is Adela in?' he asked with a grin.

'Nobody's home. Come in for a moment. I'll show you my drawings.'

'If there's no one in, then I won't deny myself the pleasure. Open the door.'

Glancing quickly to both sides like a thief, he stepped inside.

4.

'These are wonderful drawings,' he said, holding them away from himself with the air of a connoisseur. His face brightened with reflections of colours and lights. A few times he curled his hand around his eye and peered through this improvised telescope, twisting his features into a grimace filled with gravity and discernment.

'One might say,' he continued, 'that the world had passed through your hands in order to renew itself, to moult or shed its skin like a magical lizard. Do you think I would steal and commit a thousand insanities if the world were not so thoroughly worn out and impoverished, if the things of the world had not lost their lustre, the distant reflection of divine hands? For what can one do in such a world? How does one not lose heart and fall into despair, when everything is shut up tight, its meaning walled up, and everywhere you can only knock against brick, like the walls of a prison? Ah, Józef, you should have been born earlier!'

We stood there in that dim, deep room, which extended in perspective towards the window onto the market square. From out there, the waves of air reached us in gentle pulses that spread in silence. Each influx brought a new cargo seasoned with faraway colours, as if the previous one were already worn out and exhausted. The dark room lived only by the reflections of the distant houses outside the window, mirroring their colours in its depths like a camera obscura. Through the window, the pigeons on the police guard-house could be seen as if through the tube of a telescope, feathers puffed out, strutting along the cornice of the attic. Sometimes they all took flight together, describing a semicircle in the air over the square. Then, for a moment, the room became bright with their open flight feathers, flaring up with the reflected light of their distant fluttering, before fading again as they closed their wings on descent.

'To you, Szloma,' I said, 'I can reveal the secret of my drawings. From the very beginning, I have been visited by doubts as to whether I am truly their author. Sometimes they seem to me like unconscious plagiarisms, something whispered or suggested to me . . . As if some alien thing had made use of my inspiration for purposes unknown to me. For I must confess to you,' I added softly, looking him in the eye, 'that I have found the Authentic . . .'

'The Authentic?' he asked, his face brightened by a sudden light.

'Just so. See for yourself,' I said, kneeling down beside an open drawer.

I took out a silk dress belonging to Adela, a box of ribbons, and her new high-heeled slippers. The scent of powder and perfume hung in the air. I picked up a pile of books: at the bottom was none other than my long-forgotten, precious sheaf of tattered papers, glowing in the half-light.

'Szloma,' I said with emotion. 'Look, there it is . . .'

But he stood lost in meditation, Adela's shoe in his hand, studying it with profound concentration.

'This, God did not say,' he declared. 'And yet how deeply it persuades me, pinning me down and taking away all my arguments. These lines are irrefutable, shockingly incisive, conclusive, striking like lightning to the very heart of the matter. For how can you defend yourself or resist when you have already been bribed, outvoted, and betrayed by your most loyal allies? Six days of the creation were divine and bright. But on the seventh day, He sensed an alien element under his hands. Terrified, He withdrew his hands from the world, though His creative fervour had been ordained for many more days and nights. O, Joseph, beware the seventh day . . .'

Raising Adela's slender shoe in horror, as if bewitched by the shiny, ironic eloquence of that empty husk of lacquer, he said: 'Do you understand the monstrous cynicism of this symbol on a woman's foot, the provocation of her dissipated steps on these exquisite heels? How could I leave you under the power of this symbol! God forbid that I should do such a thing . . .'

At that, he deftly slipped Adela's shoes, dress, and beads under his coat.

'What are you doing, Szloma?' I asked, stupefied.

But he was already moving rapidly towards the door, limping slightly in his short, chequered trousers. In the doorway, he turned his grey, indistinct face once more, raising his hand to his lips in a reassuring gesture. And then he was gone.

MY FATHER JOINS
THE FIRE BRIGADE

I N THE FIRST days of October, we returned with
Mother from a summer resort in the neighbouring
province of our country, in the forested basin of the
Słotwinka River—a region permeated with the springy
murmur of a thousand streams. With our ears still
filled with the rustle of alders interlaced with the
chirping of birds, we travelled in a large old landau
carriage, its enormous hood bulging like a dark, roomy
inn, squashed in among our bundles in its deep, velvet-
lined alcove, while colourful images of the landscape
fell in through the window, page by page, as if shuffled
slowly from one hand to another.

Towards evening, we came to a windswept
plateau—a vast, astonished crossroads of the country.
The sky hung deep and inspired above those crossroads, revolving at its zenith in the colourful rose of
the winds. This was the most distant tollgate of the

country, the final bend before the expansive, late landscape of autumn opened up down below. Here was the border, and here stood an old, rotten border post with a faded sign playing in the wind.

The great wheel rims of the landau grated and dug into the sand; the chatter of the flashing spokes died away; only the great hood dully resounded as it flapped darkly in the crosswinds like the ark stranded in the wilderness.

Mother paid the toll, the tollgate boom creaked up, and the landau drove heavily into the autumn.

We drove into the withered boredom of a great plain, into a pale and faded blusteriness that opened its blissful, vapid infinity over the yellow horizon. A late, towering eternity arose from that faded horizon, blowing across the plain.

Like an old romance novel, the yellowed pages of the landscape turned ever paler and ever more insipid, as if they were to meet their end in some great dissipated void. In that dispersed nothingness, in that yellow nirvana, we could have driven on beyond all time and reality, staying forever in that landscape, in that warm, barren blowing of the wind—a motionless stagecoach on enormous wheels, stuck amidst the clouds on the parchment of the sky, an old illustration, a forgotten woodcut in a quaint, scattered romance—when suddenly the coachman yanked on the reins with the last of his strength, steering the landau out of the sweet lethargy of those winds and turning into a forest.

We drove into a thick, dry fluffiness, a tobacco-like shrivelling. Soon it was as cosy and brown around us as the inside of a box of Trabucos. In that cedar semi-darkness, we clattered past trunks of trees as dry and fragrant as cigars. As we drove, the wood became darker and darker, smelling ever more aromatically of snuff, until at last it locked us in, as if inside the dry body of a cello that the wind had dully tuned. The coachman did not have any matches, so he could not light the lantern. The horses panted in the darkness, finding their way by instinct. The clatter of the spokes slowed down and became muted, as the wheel rims turned softly through fragrant pine needles. Mother fell asleep. Time passed, unaccounted, forming strange knots and abbreviations in its flow. The darkness was impenetrable and the dry soughing of the forest roared over the hood, when suddenly the ground hardened beneath the hooves of the horses into a cobbled road; the carriage turned on the spot and came to a halt. It stopped so close to a wall that it almost scraped against it. Across from the open door of the landau, my mother was groping about for the front door to our building. The coachman was unloading our bundles.

We entered the great, branching entrance hall. It was dark, warm, and cosy, like an empty old bakery after the oven has been put out in the morning, or a bathhouse late at night as the abandoned tubs and pails cool off in the dark in a silence measured out by drips. A cricket was patiently unpicking illusory stitches of light from the darkness, a faint thread from which it did not grow any brighter. We felt our way to the stairs.

When we had reached a creaky landing at a corner, my mother said: 'Wake up, Józef. You're dropping on your feet. Only a few more steps now.' Senseless with sleepiness, I nestled more closely into her and fell fast asleep.

I could never find out from Mother afterwards how much had been real of what I had seen that night—through closed eyelids, overcome with drowsiness, falling into silent oblivion—and how much had been the fruit of my imagination.

A great debate was unfolding between Father, Mother, and Adela, the protagonist of the scene—a debate of fundamental importance, as I now surmise. If it is in vain that I guess at its still elusive meaning, then the fault lies with certain gaps in my memory, the blank spots of sleep, which I strive to fill with guesswork, supposition, and hypothesis. Dazed and unconscious, I kept drifting off into dull oblivion, while the breath of the starry night, scattered across the open window, fell upon my lowered eyelids. The night breathed in pure pulsations and then suddenly threw down a transparent curtain of stars, peering down from on high into my sleep with its old, eternal face. The ray of a distant star trapped in my eyelashes spilt its silver over the blind whites of my eyes; through the crack between my eyelids, I could see the room in the light of a candle tangled in a muddle of golden lines and zigzags.

Perhaps the whole scene really took place at some other time. There is much evidence to suggest that I witnessed it only some time later, when we returned home one day after closing up the shop with Mother and the shop assistants.

On the threshold of our apartment, Mother let out a cry of astonishment and delight, while the shop assistants were dumbstruck with awe. In the middle of the room stood a splendid brass knight, a veritable Saint George, made enormous by a cuirass, the gold bucklers of his spaulders, and the whole jingling paraphernalia of polished gold plate. With admiration and joy, I recognized the bristling moustache and beard of my father sticking out from beneath the heavy praetorian helmet. The breastplate rippled on his agitated chest, and the brass rings breathed through the gaps like the body of an enormous insect. Augmented by his armour in the gleam of golden metal, he looked like the Prince of the Heavenly Host.

'Sadly, Adela,' said Father, 'you have never had any understanding of matters of the higher spheres. Everywhere and always you have thwarted my plans with your outbursts of mindless anger. But now, clad in armour, I laugh in the face of your tickling, which once brought me, defenceless, to the brink of despair. Helpless fury now moves your tongue to a pathetic volubility whose crudeness and vulgarity is mixed with dim-wittedness. Believe me when I say that it fills me only with sadness and pity. Devoid of any noble flights of fantasy, you burn with unconscious hatred for everything elevated above the commonplace.'

Adela looked Father up and down, her eyes filled with utter contempt. She turned to Mother with an agitated air, weeping tears of annoyance in spite of herself: 'He's taking all our juice! He's taking all the demijohns of raspberry juice that we cooked up together in the summer! He wants to give it all to those wastrel pompiers. And to make matters worse he has been showering me with impertinences.' She sobbed briefly. 'Captain of the fire brigade—captain of the bandits, more like it!' she cried, aiming a baleful look at Father. 'The place is crawling with them. In the morning, when I want to pop out to the bakery, I can't even get through the door. Two of them have fallen asleep on the threshold in the hallway, blocking the exit. On the staircase, there's one lying on each step, fast asleep in their brass helmets. They invite themselves into the kitchen, shoving their rabbity faces in those brass cans of theirs through the crack in the door, sticking up two fingers like schoolchildren and whining imploringly "sugar, sugar" . . . They tear the bucket out of my hands and run off to carry the water, dancing and simpering around me, as if they were wagging their tails. And all the while they leer at me with red eyelids, licking their lips repulsively. It's enough for me just to glance at one of them for his face to puff up in red, shameless flesh like a turkey. Imagine giving our raspberry juice to them!'

'Your vulgar nature,' said Father, 'defiles everything it touches. You have sketched out an image of these sons of fire worthy only of your own vapid mind. As for me, all my sympathies lie with that unhappy breed of salamanders, with those poor, disinherited creatures of fire. The only fault of that once magnificent breed lay in their submission to human service, that they sold themselves to men for a teaspoon of miserable human fare. They have been repaid with contempt. The dim-wittedness of the plebs is boundless. Those delicate creatures have been led into the deepest decline, into total degradation. Is it any wonder that they do not care for the bland, vulgar provender prepared in a communal cauldron by the school caretaker's wife for them and the town prisoners? Their palate—the delicate and prodigious palate of fire spirits—demands dark and noble balms, aromatic and colourful fluids. And so on that festive evening, when we shall all sit in celebration in the great hall of the town's Stauropegion Institute at a table laid in white, in that hall with its high, brightly illuminated windows throwing their light out into the depths of the autumn night, as the town outside teems with thousands of lights, then each of us will dip his bread roll into a cup of raspberry juice with the piety and discernment so characteristic of the sons of fire, slowly sipping the thick and noble liqueur. In this manner, the inner essence of the fireman is restored, regenerating the richness of colours that the whole tribe projects in the form of fireworks, rockets, and Bengal lights. My soul is filled with pity for their misery, for their guiltless degradation. If I have accepted from their hands the captain's sabre, it is only in the hope that I might succeed in lifting the tribe out of its decline, leading it out of humiliation and unfolding above them the banner of a new idea.'

'You are entirely transformed, Jakub,' said Mother. 'You are magnificent. But you won't be going anywhere tonight. We haven't even had the chance to talk since my return. As for the pompiers,' she said, turning to Adela, 'it does seem to me that you are motivated by prejudice. They are nice boys, even if they are wastrels. It is always a delight to behold those slender young men in their fetching uniforms, just a little too tight at the waist. They have a great deal of natural elegance about them, and it is touching to see the ardour and enthusiasm with which they are ready to wait on the ladies at the drop of a hat. Whenever my parasol slips from my hand on the street or the ribbon of my shoe comes undone, one of them always comes running, filled with fervent solicitude and eagerness. I haven't the heart to disappoint their ardent intentions, and so I always wait patiently for him to reach me and come to my aid, which seems to make him very glad. As he walks away after the commission of his knightly duty, he is surrounded at once by the gang of his companions, who engage him in lively discussion about the whole incident, prompting the hero to re-enact it in mime. If I were you, I would make the most of their gallantry.'

'I regard them as freeloaders,' said Teodor, the senior shop assistant. 'After all, we don't even allow

them to put out fires because of their childish irre-
sponsibility. It's enough to see how enviously they stop
before a group of boys tossing buttons against a wall to
judge the maturity of their rabbit-like minds. When
the wild shriek of play echoes in from the street, you
can be almost certain when you look out the window
to see those beanpoles charging about among the
whole gang of boys, entirely preoccupied, almost
unconscious in the clamour of the chase. At the sight
of a fire, they go mad with joy, clapping their hands
and dancing like savages. No, they're no use for putting
out fires. We use the chimney sweeps and municipal
police for that. Which only leaves games and folk festi-
vals—in which they are unrivalled. For example, in the
so-called storming of the Capitol, at the crack of dawn
in autumn, they dress up as Carthaginians and lay
siege to the Basilian hill with an infernal uproar. Then
they all sing *Hannibal, Hannibal ante portas*.

'Towards the end of autumn, they become lazy
and languid, falling asleep on their feet. By the time
the first snow falls, they can't be found for love or
money. A certain old stove fitter once told me that
while repairing chimneys he finds them attached to
the inside of the flue, rigid as chrysalises in their red
uniforms and shiny helmets. They sleep upright like
that, drunk on raspberry juice, their insides filled with

sticky sweetness and fire. Then he hauls them out by their ears and marches them back to their barracks, drunk with sleep and unconscious, through autumn morning streets coloured with the first light frost, while the passing street rabble throw stones at them, and they grin their embarrassed grins, filled with guilt and bad conscience, staggering along like drunkards.'

'In any case,' said Adela, 'I'm not giving them any juice. I didn't ruin my complexion in the kitchen boiling it up so that those wastrels could drink it all.'

Instead of answering, my father raised a whistle to his lips and blew it hysterically. As if they had been listening at the keyhole, four slender youths burst in and lined up against the wall. The room brightened with the gleam of their helmets, while they stood to attention, dark and tanned under their bright basci-nets, awaiting orders. At Father's signal, two of them took hold of each side of a large wicker-encased demi-john, filled with purple fluid, and, before Adela could stop them, they raced down the stairs with a clatter, carrying off the precious loot. The remaining two made military bows and then disappeared after the others.

For a moment, it seemed that Adela might be roused to an act of insanity, such was the fire that had engulfed her beautiful eyes. But Father did not wait for the eruption of her anger. In a single bound, he reached the windowsill and spread his arms. We ran after him. The market square was brightly sown with lights and teeming with colourful crowds. Beneath our building, eight firemen had stretched a huge sailcloth out into a circle. Father turned back to us once more, shining in all the glory of his armour, silently saluted us, and then, with arms outstretched, as bright as a meteor, he leapt out into the night, which burned with a thousand lights. It was such a beautiful sight that all of us clapped our hands in delight. Even Adela, forgetting her rancour, applauded the leap, performed with such elegance. My father hopped down jauntily from the sheet, jangled his metal carapace, and took his place at the head of the squad, which marched off in twos in a long, winding column that slowly disappeared down a dark channel through the crowd, the brass tins of their helmets shining.

THE SANATORIUM
UNDER THE HOURGLASS

I.

T HE JOURNEY WAS long. Only a handful of
passengers travelled on that forgotten branch
line, where the trains ran but once a week. I had never
seen such old-fashioned wagons, long since retired
from the other lines—as spacious as rooms, dark, filled
with nooks and crannies. Those corridors bending at
various angles and the empty compartments, labyrinthine and cold, had something strangely abandoned
about them, something almost terrifying. I wandered
from wagon to wagon in search of a cosy corner.
Everywhere was draughty, as the cold air blew through
those interiors, boring right through the train. People
sat here and there on the floor with their bundles, not
daring to occupy the empty benches, which were
unusually high. In any case, those bulging oilskin seats

were as cold as ice and sticky with age. At the empty stations, not a single passenger boarded. Without so much as a whistle or a puff, the train slowly set off again on its onward journey, as if in deep contemplation.

For a time, I was accompanied by a man in a torn railwayman's uniform, silent and lost in thought. He pressed a handkerchief to his sore, swollen face. Then he too disappeared, disembarking unnoticed at some stop or other. He left behind an empty space pressed into the straw that covered the floor, and a battered black suitcase, which he had forgotten.

Wading through the straw and refuse, I moved in tottering steps from wagon to wagon. The doors to the compartments wobbled in the draught, gaping wide open. There was not a passenger to be seen. At last, I met a conductor in the black uniform of the railway service of that line. He was wrapping a thick scarf around his neck and packing up his gear, his torch, and his official notebook. 'We're arriving, sir,' he said, looking at me with white eyes. The train slowly came to a halt, without any puffing or rattling, as if the life were ebbing out of it together with the last breath of steam. We stopped. Silence and emptiness. No station building. As he got out, he pointed me in the direction of the Sanatorium.

With suitcase in hand, I set off along a narrow white road that soon disappeared into the dark thickets of a park. With a certain curiosity, I looked round at the landscape. The road I was following climbed up to the ridge of a small rise from which one could take in the whole horizon. The day was grey, muted, and featureless. Perhaps under the influence of that heavy, colourless aura, the great bowl of the horizon darkened, its vast, forested landscape arranging itself, as if on the wings of a stage, from strips and layers of forestation, ever more distant and ever greyer, falling in streaks and gentle slopes from both sides. The whole of that dark landscape, filled with solemnity, seemed almost imperceptibly to flow into itself, to slide past itself like a cloudy, banked-up sky filled with hidden movement. The fluid belts and trails of the forests seemed to murmur, and then to swell in that murmuring like a tide rising imperceptibly towards the land. Amidst the dark dynamics of the forested terrain, the raised white path meandered like a melody along a ridge of wide chords, squeezed by the pressure of the mighty musical masses that would eventually swallow it up. I plucked a branch from a roadside tree. The green of the leaves was dark, almost black. It was a strangely vivid blackness, deep and benevolent like a dream filled with nourishment and power. All the greys of the landscape were derived from that single shade. In our region, the landscape takes on that hue on a cloudy summer's evening saturated with persistent rain. The same deep, calm abnegation, the same resigned and definitive numbness, no longer in need of the consolation of colour.

In the forest, it was as dark as night. I groped my way forward over the quiet needles. When the trees thinned out, I heard the boards of a bridge rattling beneath my feet. On the other side, amidst the darkness of the trees, loomed the grey, many-windowed wall of the hotel advertising itself as the Sanatorium. The glass double doors of its entrance were open. One entered straight from the bridge, which was lined on both sides by rickety balustrades made of birch branches. In the corridor, semi-darkness and a solemn silence reigned. I tiptoed from door to door, reading out the numbers on them in the gloom. At a corner, I finally met a chambermaid. She was dashing out of a room, as if she had just extricated herself from somebody's importunate hands, breathless and agitated. She could barely comprehend what I said to her. I had to repeat myself. She fidgeted nervously.

Had they received my telegram? She threw up her hands, her eyes darting to one side. She was just waiting for the chance to slip away through the half-open door on which her gaze was fixed.

'I have come from far away. I booked a room in this hotel by telegram,' I said, with a certain impatience. 'Who can I speak to about this?'

She did not know. 'Perhaps you can wait in the restaurant, sir,' she stammered. 'Everyone is sleeping now. When the doctor gets up, I'll check you in.'

'Sleeping? But it's daytime, and still a long time before night . . .'

'Here they're always sleeping. Didn't you know?' she asked, lifting her eyes in curiosity. 'In any case, it's never night here,' she added coquettishly. She no longer wanted to flee, picking at the lace of her apron as she stood there.

I left her. I entered the restaurant, which was half in darkness. There were tables and a great buffet that took up the length of an entire wall. For the first time in a long while, I felt the pangs of a certain appetite. I was pleased at the sight of the pastries and cakes heaped plentifully on the plates of the buffet.

I laid my suitcase down on one of the tables. They were all empty. I clapped my hands. No response. I peeked into the next room, which was larger and brighter. The room opened out through a wide window or loggia onto the now familiar landscape, which in the frame of the window casing looked like a funeral memorial in all its sadness and resignation. On the tablecloths were the remains of a recent meal, with uncorked bottles and half-drained glasses. Here and there were even some gratuities, as yet uncollected by the serving staff. I went back to the buffet, examining the cakes and pâtés. They all looked exceedingly tasty. I wondered whether it would be impolite to serve myself. I felt the rush of a prodigious craving. In particular, the sight of crumbly cakes with apple marmalade had my mouth watering. I was just about to prise one up with a silver server when I sensed someone's presence behind me. The chambermaid approached on her soft slippers and touched my back with her fingers. 'The Doctor will see you,' she said, inspecting her fingernails.

She walked in front of me, never looking back, certain of the magnetism produced by the play of her hips. She toyed with the intensity of that magnetism, regulating the distance between our bodies as we passed dozens of numbered doors. The corridor became darker and darker. Now in total darkness, she brushed fleetingly against me. 'Here is the Doctor's room,' she whispered. 'Please enter.'

Doctor Gotard greeted me standing in the middle of the room. He was a rather short man, broad-shouldered with a black beard.

'We received your telegram yesterday,' he said. 'We sent the company coach to the station, but you arrived by a different train. Unfortunately, the rail connection isn't the best here. How do you feel?'

'Is my father alive?' I asked, shooting an anxious look at his smiling face.

'He's alive, naturally,' he replied, calmly holding my ardent gaze. 'Of course, within the limits imposed by his situation,' he added, narrowing his eyes. 'You know as well as I that from the point of view of your home, from the perspective of your homeland, your father has already died. This cannot be entirely undone. His death throws a certain shadow on his existence here.'

'But Father doesn't know? He doesn't guess?' I asked in a whisper. He shook his head with deep conviction. 'You may be assured,' he said in a lowered voice, 'that our patients do not guess, that they cannot guess . . .'

'The whole trick,' he added, ready to demonstrate the mechanism on his fingers, 'is that we have turned back time. We are late in time here by a certain interval, the length of which is difficult to determine. It all comes down to simple relativity. Here your father's death has simply not yet occurred—I mean, the death that has already reached him in your homeland.'

'But in that case,' I said, 'Father is dying or at death's door . . .'

'You misunderstand, sir,' he replied in a tone of indulgent impatience. 'We have reactivated past time with all its possibilities here—which also means the possibility of recovery.'

He stared at me with a smile, stroking his beard.

'But now you would like to see your father, I'm sure. In accordance with your instructions, we have reserved a bed for you in his room. I will take you there now.'

Once we were out in the dark corridor, Doctor Gotard spoke in a whisper. I noticed that he was wearing felt slippers, like the chambermaid.

'We allow our patients to sleep a lot in order to conserve their life force. In any case, they don't have anything better to do around here.'

Finally, he stopped at a door. He put his finger to his lips.

'Please go in quietly—your father is sleeping. You should lie down too. It would be the best thing for you to do at the moment. Goodbye.'

'Goodbye,' I whispered, feeling the beating of my heart in my throat. I turned the handle; the door opened by itself, swinging ajar like a mouth gaping helplessly in sleep. I stepped inside. The room was almost empty, grey and bare. On an ordinary wooden bed under a small window, my father lay covered in voluminous bedclothes, fast asleep. His deep breathing released whole seams of snoring from the depths of his slumber. The room seemed to be lined with his snores, from floor to ceiling, as new layers kept accumulating. Filled with emotion, I stared at the haggard, emaciated face of my father, now entirely absorbed by the labour of his snoring—a face in a distant trance, having thrown off its earthly shell, confessing its existence somewhere on that remote shore through the solemn counting of its minutes.

There was no other bed. A penetrating chill blew in from the window. The stove was not lit.

'They don't seem too concerned about the patients,' I thought to myself. 'Such a sick man left to the mercy of the draughts! And it looks like nobody cleans around here either. The floor and the nightstand, with its medicines and glass of cold coffee, are covered with a thick layer of dust. There are piles of cakes in the restaurant, and yet they give the patients black coffee instead of something more nourishing! Still, I suppose in comparison with the benefits of turned-back time these are mere trifles.'

I slowly undressed and slipped into my father's bed. He did not wake up. His snoring, apparently now banked up too high, dropped down an octave, resigning from the previous grandiloquence of its declamations. It became a kind of private snoring for its own use. I tucked the eiderdown in around my father, protecting him as far as possible from the draught blowing in from the window. Soon I fell asleep beside him.

2.

When I awoke, it was dark in the room. Father was sitting at the table, already dressed, drinking tea and dunking frosted biscuits in it. He was wearing the new black clothes of English cloth that he had bought himself the year before. His necktie was somewhat carelessly fastened.

Seeing that I was awake, he smiled pleasantly, still slightly pale with his illness: 'I'm so glad you have come, Józef. What a surprise! I've been so lonely here. Of course, I shouldn't complain—I've been through much worse things, and if one wanted to take the *facit* from every situation . . . But enough about that. Just imagine—on my first day here they served me a magnificent *filet de boeuf* with mushrooms. What an infernal piece of meat it was, Józef! I warn you most strenuously—if they ever try to serve you *filet de boeuf* here . . . I can still feel the fire in my belly. Diarrhoea and still more diarrhoea . . . I couldn't stomach it at all. But I must give you some news,' he continued. 'Don't laugh. I've rented space for a shop here. That's right. I'm quite proud of the idea. I was bored, you see, terribly bored. You can't imagine what boredom reigns here. But at least now I have something pleasant to keep me occupied. Don't imagine anything special. Not at all. A far more modest place than our old shop. A mere shed in comparison. Back in town, we'd be ashamed of such a measly little market stall, but here we've had to lower our standards a bit, haven't we, Józef?' He smiled weakly. 'Somehow one manages to live.' I began to feel sorry for him and ashamed at his confusion as he realized he had used the wrong word.

'I see you're still sleepy,' he said, after a pause. 'Sleep a little longer, and then you can visit me at the shop, can't you? I need to dash over there now to see how business is going. You have no idea how difficult it was to get any credit, how suspiciously they treat old merchants with a serious history . . . Do you remember the optician's on the market square? Our shop is right next door. There's still no sign, but you'll find it. You can't miss it.'

'Are you going out without your coat, Father?' I asked anxiously.

'I forgot to pack it. Can you imagine? I couldn't find it in my trunk, but I haven't needed it at all. The climate is so mild here, and the air so sweet!'

'Take my coat, Father,' I insisted. 'Please do take it.' But Father had already put on his hat. He waved his hand at me and slipped out of the room.

I wasn't sleepy anymore. I felt rested ... and hungry. I recalled with relish the buffet stacked with cakes. I got dressed, thinking of how I would indulge myself with the many varieties of those delicacies. I intended to start with the apple crumble, without neglecting the magnificent sponge cake filled with orange sauce. I stood in front of the looking glass to put on my tie, but its surface, like a curved mirror, seemed to conceal my image within it, swirling in its murky depths. In vain, I adjusted my distance from it, approaching and backing away, but the fluid, silvery mist did not want to reveal a reflection. I'll have to tell them to get me another mirror, I thought to myself, as I went out of the room.

The corridor was dark. The impression of solemn silence was intensified by the faint light of a gas lamp burning with a blueish flame at a corner. In that laby-rinth of doors, casings, and recesses, it was difficult to find the entrance to the restaurant. 'I'll head out into town,' I thought, with sudden resolution. 'I'll eat somewhere there, and perhaps find a decent cake shop.'

As soon as I stepped outside, I was shrouded in the heavy, moist, sweet air of that peculiar climate. The chronic greyness of the atmosphere descended by a few more tones. It was as if one were seeing the day through a funeral pall.

I drank in the sight of the velvety, juicy blackness of the darkest parts, the scale of subdued greys and plush ashes, running down through passages of muted tones restrained by the damper of the keyboard—that nocturne of the landscape. The heavy, billowing air flapped about my face in soft sheets. It had the sickly sweetness of standing rainwater.

Again, the soughing of the black woods, echoing back upon itself in dull chords, churning up space beyond the range of audibility! I was in the rear court-yard of the Sanatorium. I looked round at the high walls of the annexe to the main building, bending round in a horseshoe shape. All the windows were closed behind black shutters. The Sanatorium was fast asleep. I passed a gate of metal railings. Beside it stood a dog kennel of unusual proportions, apparently abandoned. Once again, I was swallowed up and embraced by the black forest, groping my way into its darkness as if with my eyes closed on the quiet needles. As the light slowly grew, the shapes of houses emerged between the trees. A few more steps and I found myself in a vast town square.

What a strange and misleading resemblance to the market square of our own native town! How similar all the squares of the world must be! Almost the very same houses and shops!

The pavements were nearly empty. The funereal, late half-light of an indeterminate time of day filtered down from a sky of undefined greyness. I could easily make out all the posters and signs, and yet I wouldn't have been surprised if I had been told it was the dead of night. Only a few shops were open. The others had their shutters half lowered, as if they had closed in a hurry. The thick, luxuriant air, intoxicating and rich, swallowed up the view here and there, wiping away a few houses, a lamp post, and part of a sign, like a wet sponge. At times, it was difficult even to open one's eyelids, which drooped in a strange lassitude or drowsiness. I began to search for the optician's shop my father had mentioned. He had spoken about it as something familiar to me, appealing to my local knowledge. Did he not know I was visiting for the first time? Things had clearly become confused in his mind. But then what else could be expected of a father who was only half-real himself, living a life that was conditional, relative, and limited by so many caveats! It was hard to ignore that one needed a great deal of goodwill to grant him any kind of existence at all. It was a pitiful, surrogate life, dependent on a universal indulgence, on that *consensus omnium* from which it drew its insipid juices. Indeed, it was thanks only to that sympathetic peeking through one's fingers, the collective turning of a blind eye to the obvious and glaring deficiencies of that state of things, that he could preserve a pathetic pretence of life for a little while in the fabric of reality. The slightest resistance might shake him and the weakest gust of scepticism throw him down. Could Doctor Gotard's Sanatorium really provide him with that hothouse atmosphere of kindly tolerance, protecting him from the cold gusts of sobriety and critique? One had to marvel that in the midst of this dubious and endangered state of things my father could still maintain such a resplendent bearing.

I was pleased to see the display window of a cake shop filled with cakes and sweets. My appetite revived. I opened the glass door with a sign saying 'ice cream' and entered the dark shop. It smelt of coffee and vanilla. A young lady emerged from the depths of the shop, her face blurred by the darkness. She took my order. Finally, after all this time, I could restore myself, taking my fill of plump doughnuts, which I dunked in my coffee. In the gloom, with the whirling arabesques of dusk dancing around me, I wolfed down one cake after another, as the swirling darkness forced its way under my eyelids, stealthily infesting my insides with its warm pulsations in a swarm of delicate touches. At last, only the rectangle of the window glowed as a grey stain in the total darkness. In vain, I tapped a teaspoon on the table top. Nobody appeared to take payment for my meal. I left a silver coin on the table and stepped out onto the street. The bookshop next door was still illuminated. The shop assistants were busy sorting books. I asked about my father's shop. 'It's the shop right next door to us,' they informed me. An obliging young lad even ran to the door to show me. The vestibule was glass; the display window was not yet ready, still covered in grey paper. From the doorway, I noticed with surprise that the shop was filled with customers. My father stood behind the counter, licking his pencil as he added up the items of a long bill. The gentleman for whom he was preparing it traced out every figure with his index finger, counting under his breath as he leant against the counter. The rest of the customers looked on in silence. My father darted a glance at me from under his spectacles, holding his finger on the item at which he had paused: 'There's a letter for you on the desk among the papers.' Then he plunged back into his counting. Meanwhile, the shop assistants were putting aside the purchased items, wrapping them in paper, and tying them up with string. The shelves were only partly filled with cloth. Most of them were still empty.

'Why don't you sit down, Father?' I asked quietly, slipping behind the counter. 'You aren't looking after yourself at all—and in your condition.' He waved his hand, as if to dismiss my pleas, and kept on counting. He looked haggard. It was as clear as day that only this artificial excitement, this fevered activity, was sustaining him, putting off for another moment the inevitable collapse.

I searched through the papers on the desk. It was more of a package than a letter. A few days earlier I had written to a bookshop in the matter of a certain pornographic book, and now it had been sent to me here. They had found my address, or rather Father's address, even though he had only just opened the shop, which still lacked a sign or company name. It really was an astonishing effort of investigation, showing admirable efficiency on the part of the delivery service! And with such speed!

'You can read it out back in the office,' said Father, shooting an irritated glance at me. 'You can see your-self that there's no room here.'

The office behind the shop was still empty. A little light filtered through the glass door from inside. The assistants' coats were hanging on the walls. I opened the package and began to read in the feeble light from the doorway.

I was informed that the requested book was regret-tably out of stock. A search for it had begun, but with no guarantee of its outcome the company had taken the liberty in the meantime of sending me a certain item, no strings attached, which they anticipated would be of great interest to me. What followed was a convoluted description of a collapsible astronomical refracting telescope of great illuminating power and with many special features. Intrigued, I took the instru-ment out of the envelope—it was made of black oilcloth or stiff canvas folded up into a flat concertina. I had always had a soft spot for telescopes. I began to unfold the multiple pleats of the instrument's cover. Stiffened by slender rods, the enormous bellows of the telescope unfolded in my hands, so that its empty hood stretched out to the length of the entire room in a labyrinth of black chambers, a long confabulation of lightproof boxes half tucked into one another. It almost took the form of a long automobile made of lacquered canvas, a theatre prop imitating in light, paper material and stiff cloth the sturdy mass of reality. I looked into the black funnel of the eyepiece and saw in its depths the faint outline of the courtyard façade of the Sanatorium. Intrigued, I slipped further into the back chamber of the apparatus. Now I saw the chambermaid in the telescope's field of vision, as she walked down a canvas corridor in the Sanatorium with a tray in her hand. She turned round and smiled. 'Can she see me?' I thought to myself. An overwhelming drowsiness veiled my eyes in a fog. I was now seated in the back chamber of the telescope as if in a limousine. With a slight movement of a lever, the whole apparatus began to rustle with the flapping sound of a paper butterfly; I felt it move with me inside it, turning towards the door.

Like a great, black caterpillar, the telescope drove out onto the illuminated shop floor—a segmented body, an enormous paper cockroach with two imitation headlights on its front. The shoppers crowded together as they backed away before that blind paper dragon. The shop assistants opened the door onto the street, and I slowly drove outside in my paper automobile between the rows of customers, who watched that truly scandalous departure with shocked faces.

3.

And so life goes in this town, as time passes by. For most of the day, one sleeps—and not only in bed. No, one cannot be too fussy on that point. In any place and at any time of day, a person is ready for a nap here. With his head down on a table in a restaurant, in a carriage, even on his feet on the street or in the entrance hall to a house he has just visited for a moment only to surrender to the irresistible need to sleep.

On waking, still befuddled and hazy, we carry on our interrupted conversation, continuing down our arduous road, pursuing that intricate affair without beginning or end. As a result, whole intervals of time are lost along the way, and we lose control over the continuity of the day. In the end, we stop worrying about it, abandoning without regret the skeleton of unbroken chronology to whose attentive supervision we had once been so accustomed from sheer force of habit or from conscientious everyday discipline. We have long since sacrificed that constant readiness to account for lived time, that scrupulousness in counting the spent hours down to the last penny—the pride and glory of our economy. From these cardinal virtues, in which we had once known neither hesitation nor deviation, we have long since capitulated.

A few examples may serve to illustrate this state of affairs. At some time of day or night—distinguishable only by a barely visible nuance of the sky—I wake up by the balustrade of the little bridge leading to the Sanatorium. It is dusk. Overcome by drowsiness, I must have wandered unconsciously around the town before dragging myself, terminally exhausted, to the bridge. I cannot say for sure whether I had been accompanied the whole time by Doctor Gotard, who now stands beside me, concluding a lengthy disquisition. Carried away by his own eloquence, he seizes me by the arm and tugs me along after him. I go with him, but before we have even crossed the rattling boards of the bridge I am asleep again. Through closed eyelids, I can still hazily see the Doctor's astute gesticulations and the smile in the depths of his black beard as I struggle in vain to comprehend the splendid flourish of his logic, the final trump card with which he now triumphs, halting with folded arms at the culmination of his arguments. I do not know how long we walk like that, side by side, immersed in a conversation filled with misunderstandings, when suddenly I wake up properly, Doctor Gotard is no longer there, and it is completely dark—but only because my eyes are closed. I open them and find myself in bed, in my room, without knowing how I got there.

An even more drastic example:

I enter a restaurant in town at lunchtime, stepping into the chaotic hubbub and commotion of the diners. And whom should I meet there in the middle of the room at a table creaking under the weight of numerous dishes? Father. All eyes are fixed on him, as he turns affectedly to all sides, extraordinarily animated, ecstatic, his diamond pin shining, in effusive conversation with the whole room at once. With an artificial bravado that I cannot observe without anxiety, he orders one dish after another, stacking them up in piles on the table. He arranges them around him with delight, though he has not yet finished the first course. Smacking his lips, chewing, and speaking all at the same time, he feigns with gestures and facial expressions the greatest satisfaction with the whole banquet, following Adam, the waiter, with enamoured eyes and calling out new orders with an adoring smile. When the waiter comes running to fulfil them, his napkin flapping, Father appeals to everybody with an imploring gesture, summoning them all as witnesses to the irresistible charm of this Ganymede.

'Precious boy!' he cries with a blissful smile, closing his eyes. 'Angelic boy! You must confess, gentlemen, that he is charming!'

Filled with distaste, I withdraw from the room, unseen by Father. If he had been intentionally dispatched by the hotel management to entertain the guests, he could not have behaved more provocatively or ostentatiously. My head still spinning with drowsiness, I stagger on through the streets, making my way home. I rest my head on a postbox for a moment and indulge myself in a brief siesta. Finally, I grope my way in the gloom to the front door of the Sanatorium and go inside. It is dark in my room. I flick the switch, but the electricity is out. A cold draught blows in from the window. The bed creaks in the darkness. Father lifts his head up over the bedclothes: 'Ah, Józef, Józef! I've been lying here for two days without any attention. The bell has been disconnected, nobody looks in on me, and my own son abandons me, a gravely sick man, to chase girls around the town. Look how my heart thumps.'

How can this be explained? Is my father sitting in the restaurant in the grip of an unhealthy hubris of gluttony, or is he lying gravely ill in his room? Are there two fathers? Nothing of the sort. It is all a result of the rapid disintegration of time, no longer supervised under constant vigilance.

We all know that this undisciplined element can barely be kept in check even with the benefit of constant cultivation, solicitous care, and the meticulous regulation and correction of its excesses. Without such attention, it is at once inclined to fall into transgressions, wild aberrations, erratic pranks, and formless clowning. The incommensurability of our individual times becomes ever more apparent. My father's time and my own time were already no longer in agreement.

Incidentally, my father's accusations of moral dissolution are baseless innuendo. I have not so much as gone near a girl here. Stumbling along like a drunkard from one slumber to the next, I have paid scant attention to the local members of the fairer sex, even in my most lucid moments.

In any case, the chronic dusk on the streets makes it impossible to distinguish between faces. The only thing I have noticed, as a young man still not without a certain interest in the subject, is the unusual walk of the young ladies here.

They walk in unerringly straight lines, disregarding any obstacles, obedient only to some inner rhythm, some law, unravelling as if from a ball of yarn into the thread of that unwavering trot, filled with precision and a measured grace.

Each of them carries inside her a distinct, individual principle, like a wound-up spring.

As they walk straight ahead, eyes fixed on this principle, filled with concentration and solemnity, they seem to be consumed by only one care—not to miss anything, not to err in following this difficult rule, not to stray from it by even a millimetre. Then it becomes clear that what they balance over their heads with such absorption is none other than the *idée fixe* of their own perfection, which through sheer force of conviction almost becomes a reality. It is a kind of wager undertaken at their own risk, with no guarantees, an inviolable dogma elevated beyond any doubt.

What flaws and defects, what snub noses and flat ones, what pimples and freckles boldly smuggle themselves in under the flag of that fiction! There is no ugliness or vulgarity such that the enthusiasm of that faith would not lift it up into a fictional heaven of perfection.

With the sanction of that faith, the body becomes beautiful, and the legs—already shapely and supple in impeccable shoes—speak through their walk, eagerly explicating in a smooth, shimmering monologue of steps the richness of the idea that the closed face passes proudly over in silence. They keep their hands in the pockets of their short, tight-fitting jackets. In cafés and theatres, they cross their legs, exposed to the knee, and eloquently remain silent with them. But that is enough digression on but one of the town's many curiosities. I have already mentioned the dark vegetation here. Especially worthy of note is a certain species of black fern, whose enormous fronds adorn the vases in every home and every public house. It is almost a symbol of mourning, a funereal emblem of the town.

4.

Relations in the Sanatorium are becoming ever more unbearable by the day. It is hard to deny that we have simply fallen into a trap. Since the moment of my arrival, when certain appearances of solicitude were spun out before the visitor, the Sanatorium management has not made the least effort to give us even the illusion of care. We are simply left to our own devices. Nobody pays any attention to our needs. I have long maintained that the wires to the electric bells are cut off right over the door and do not lead anywhere. There is no sign of the staff. The corridors are plunged in darkness and silence, day and night. I am convinced that we are the only guests in the Sanatorium, and that the discreet, enigmatic expression with which the chambermaid closes the doors as she enters or exits the rooms is simply for show.

Sometimes I feel like opening the doors to the rooms myself, one by one, leaving them all wide open to expose the ignoble intrigue in which we have been entangled.

And yet I cannot be entirely certain of my suspicions. Sometimes late at night I see Doctor Gotard hurrying down the corridor in a white surgical gown with an enema syringe in his hand, the chambermaid rushing ahead of him. It is hard to stop him then to pin him down with a determined question.

If it weren't for the restaurant and the cake shop in town, one could starve to death here. They still haven't given us a second bed. Fresh bedding is out of the question. One would have to confess that the general slackening of standards has not spared us either.

To get into bed fully dressed, with shoes on, would once have been unthinkable to me as a civilized person. Now I come home late, drunk with somnolence, to a room veiled in semi-darkness, the sheer curtains billowing in the window in a breath of cold air. Unconscious, I collapse onto the bed and bury myself in the covers. In that position, I sleep through whole irregular spaces of time, through days and weeks, travelling across empty landscapes of sleep, ever on the road, ever on the steep highways of respiration, sometimes springing lightly down gentle slopes, and then climbing laboriously back up the perpendicular wall of slumber. Having reached the summit, I take in the vast horizons of that silent, rocky desert of sleep. At some hour, at an unknown point, somewhere at a sharp turn in my snoring, I wake up, only half conscious, and feel my father's body at my feet. He is lying there, curled up into a ball like a kitten. I fall asleep again with mouth wide open, and the whole enormous panorama of the mountainous landscape slides past me in majestic waves.

In the shop, Father is a whirlwind of activity, conducting transactions and exerting all his energy to win over the customers. His cheeks are flushed with excitement and his eyes sparkle. In the Sanatorium, he lies seriously ill, as he did in his final weeks at home. It is hard not to see that the process is rapidly approaching its fatal end. In a weak voice, he says to me: 'You should come to the shop more often, Józef. The shop assistants are stealing from us. You can see yourself that I'm not up to the task. I've been lying here ill for weeks, while the shop goes to rack and ruin, left to its fate. Were there any letters from home?'

I am beginning to regret the whole business. It is hard now to describe the idea to send Father here as a good one, seduced as we were by the grandiloquent advertisement. Time turned back ... it certainly sounded beautiful, but what did it turn out to be in reality? Does one get a wholesome, honest-to-goodness time here: time unravelled from a fresh bolt of cloth, still smelling of newness and dye? On the contrary. It is a threadbare time, a used time—ragged and full of holes, transparent as a sieve.

And no wonder, for it is a time that has been somehow regurgitated—please understand me—a second-hand time. A miserable excuse for time!

On top of all that is an entirely inappropriate manipulation of time: those shady, indecent dealings; sneaking into its mechanism from behind; recklessly fingering its delicate secrets! Sometimes one could pound the table and scream at the top of one's voice: 'Enough! Take your hands off time! Time is inviolable and not to be provoked! Are you not satisfied with space? Space is for man; you can frolic in space to your heart's content, turn somersaults, flip upside down, leap from star to star. But for the love of God, leave time alone!'

On the other hand, can I myself be expected to dissolve the contract with Doctor Gotard? However miserable my father's existence here, I can still see him. I can spend time with him; I can talk to him ...

In fact, I owe Doctor Gotard a debt of infinite gratitude.

Many times I have wanted to speak to him frankly. But Doctor Gotard is elusive. 'He just went off to the dining room,' the chambermaid informs me. I make my way over there, but she soon runs after me to say she was mistaken—Doctor Gotard is in the operating theatre. I rush upstairs, wondering what kinds of operations might be performed there. I enter the vestibule, and they tell me to wait. Doctor Gotard will be out in a moment; he has just finished an operation and is washing his hands. I almost catch a glimpse of him—diminutive, hurrying along in great strides, his cloak billowing behind him, through a suite of hospital rooms. Then what happens? It turns out that Doctor Gotard was not there at all, and that no operations have been performed here for years. Doctor Gotard is asleep in his room, his black beard pointing up into the air. The room is filled with his snoring, like banks of cloud, which swell and pile up, lifting Doctor Gotard and his bed on their mounting wisps, higher and higher: a great, pompous ascension upon waves of snoring and billowing sheets.

Even stranger things happen here, things I conceal even from myself, things fantastical in their sheer absurdity. Whenever I step out of the room, it seems to me that someone else is just hastening away from the door, turning into a side corridor. Or someone walks in front of me, never looking back. It isn't a nurse. I know who it is! 'Mama!' I call in a voice trembling with emotion. My mother turns her face to look back at me for a moment with an imploring smile. Where am I? What is happening? What tangled web have I stumbled into?

5.

I do not know whether it is the influence of the late season of the year, but the days are becoming ever more solemn in colour, clouding over and darkening. It is as if one were looking at the world through blackened spectacles.

The whole landscape is like the bottom of an immense aquarium filled with pale ink. Trees, people, and buildings blur into black silhouettes, waving like underwater plants against the background of those inky depths.

The vicinity of the Sanatorium is swarming with black dogs. Of all different shapes and sizes, they run along the roads and paths in the dusk, quietly absorbed in their doggish affairs, filled with tension and alertness.

They flash past in twos and threes, necks stuck out attentively, ears pricked up, whimpering quietly in a pathetic tone that bursts from their throats involuntarily, signalling the utmost agitation. Preoccupied with their own affairs, filled with haste, always in motion, always absorbed by an incomprehensible goal, they barely pay any attention to the passer-by. Sometimes they merely glower at him as they fly past, their wise, black eyes betraying a fury restrained only by lack of time. Sometimes they seem to indulge their anger, running up to a person's feet with head down, growling menacingly, only to abandon their intention halfway and dash off again in great doggish bounds.

There is nothing to be done about that plague of dogs, but the devil only knows why the Sanatorium management keeps an enormous Alsatian on a chain—a gruesome beast, a veritable werewolf of simply demonic ferocity.

It sends shivers down my spine every time I pass that kennel, where the beast stands motionless on a short chain, with a wildly ruffled collar of shaggy hair around its head—whiskered, bristling, bearded, the machinery of its powerful jaws filled with fangs. It does not bark at all, but its wild face becomes even more terrifying at the sight of a person, its features petrifying into an expression of fathomless fury as it slowly raises its dreadful muzzle and begins in quiet convulsions, from the depths of its hatred, a low, fervent howling, in which all the sorrow and despair of its helplessness can be heard.

My father passes the beast with indifference whenever we leave the Sanatorium together. As for me, I am shaken to the core every time I see that elemental manifestation of helpless hatred. I am now two heads taller than Father, who toddles along beside me, short and skinny, in small, senile steps.

As we approach the market square, we see an extraordinary commotion. Crowds of people are rushing through the streets. The improbable news reaches us that an enemy army has entered the town.

Amidst a general consternation, people exchange alarming and contradictory reports. It is hard to comprehend. Has the war not been preceded by any diplomatic moves? A war in the middle of a blissful peace undisturbed by any conflict? War with whom and over what? They inform us that the invasion of the enemy army has also emboldened a party of malcontents in the town, who have poured out onto the streets with weapons in hand, terrorizing the peaceful citizens. Indeed, we see a group of these terrorists in black civilian clothing, with white straps crossed over their chests, advancing in silence with rifles lowered. The crowd backs away before them, pressed together on the pavement as they walk past, shooting dark, ironic looks from under their top hats, revealing a sense of superiority, a spark of malicious amusement, a sort of conspiratorial wink, as if holding back snorts of laughter that would expose the whole mystification. Some of them are recognized by the crowd, but any cheerful greetings are suppressed by the threat of the lowered gun barrels. They pass us by without molesting anyone. Once again the streets are filled with the fearful, grimly silent crowd. A dull roar burns over the town. It seems that the rumble of artillery and the rattle of ammunition carts can be heard from afar. 'I must get through to the shop,' says my father, pale but determined. 'You don't have to go with me; you'll only get in the way,' he adds. 'Go back to the Sanatorium.' The voice of cowardice advises me to obey. I watch my father as he squeezes through the close-packed wall of the crowd, and then I lose sight of him.

I creep hurriedly along the side streets to the upper part of town. I know that on those steep streets I will be able to circumnavigate the congested centre with its human multitude.

There, in the upper part of town, the crowd became sparser, until finally it disappeared. I walked calmly along empty streets to the city park. The lanterns were burning there with a dark, blueish flame, like funereal asphodels. Around each of them danced a swarm of May bugs, heavy as balls, suspended in lateral flight on vibrating wings. Some of them had fallen to the ground and were flittering ineffectually in the sand, their hunched backs bulging in hard wing cases, under which they tried to fold away the outstretched membranes of their wings. Pedestrians strolled over the lawns and footpaths, immersed in light-hearted conversations. The last trees hung over the yards of the houses below, pressed against the park wall. I wandered along the wall, which barely reached chest height on my side, while on the other it dropped down towards the level of the yards in buttresses as high as the roofs. In a certain spot, a ramp of beaten earth rose up between the yards to the level of the wall. I leapt over the barrier with ease, then slipped down that narrow causeway between the huddled houses, back onto the street. My calculations, based on a fine spatial intuition, were correct. I found myself almost directly in front of the Sanatorium building, whose annexe glowed a hazy white within a black frame of trees.

I enter, as usual, from the back, via the courtyard, through the gate in the iron fence. I see the dog from afar at his post. As always, a shiver of aversion runs down my spine at the very sight of it. I want to pass it by as quickly as possible, so as not to have to hear that moan of hatred from the depths of its heart, when to my horror, hardly able to believe my eyes, I see it bound away from the kennel, unrestrained, and then run around the courtyard with a hollow bark that seems to have been drawn out of a barrel, apparently trying to cut off my escape.

Numb with fear, I back away into the opposite, most distant corner of the courtyard. Instinctively seeking shelter, I hide in a little summer house there, convinced of the futility of my efforts. The shaggy beast approaches in a few bounds, its muzzle now at the entrance to the summer house, shutting me in a trap. Half-dead with fear, I notice that it has already unravelled the entire length of the chain, dragging it out across the courtyard, and that the summer house is just beyond the reach of its teeth. Exhausted and shattered with terror, I barely even feel relief. Swooning, close to fainting, I raise my eyes to look at it. I have never seen it from so close and only now do the scales fall away from my eyes. How great is the power of prejudice! How powerful is the suggestion of fear! What blindness! For it was a man. A man on a chain, whom I had taken in some incomprehensible way—in a simplifying, metaphorical shortcut—for a dog. Please do not misunderstand me. He was a dog, without a shadow of a doubt. But in human form. The quality of doggishness is an inner quality and can manifest itself just as easily in human as in animal form. The one that stood before me at the entrance to the summer house—its maw peeled back, almost inside out, with all its teeth bared in a terrifying growl—was a black-bearded man of medium height. A yellow, bony face, with black eyes, angry and unhappy. Judging by his black clothing and the civilized cut of his beard, he might have been taken for a learned man or a scholar. He could have been the older, less successful brother of Doctor Gotard. Yet this first impression was misleading. His large, glue-smeared hands, the two brutal, cynical furrows around his nose, which ran down into his beard, and the vulgar, horizontal wrinkles on his forehead quickly dispelled this initial illusion. He was more likely a bookbinder, a tub-thumper, a rabble-rouser, or a party member: a violent man of dark, explosive passions. There, in the depths of his fervour, in the convulsive bristling of all his fibres, in this frenzied fury, barking wildly at the end of the stick I was pointing at him, he was one hundred per cent dog.

If I crawled out through the back of the summer house, I think to myself, I would be completely beyond the reach of his fury and could get to the gate of the Sanatorium by a side path. I am just throwing my leg over the railing when I suddenly stop in mid-motion. I sense that it would be too cruel simply to go away and leave him there, alone in his helpless, boundless fury. I imagine his dreadful disappointment, his inhuman pain, to see me escaping the trap and vanishing once and for all. I decide to stay. I approach him and speak in a calm, even voice: 'Please calm yourself, sir. I will unchain you.'

His face, chopped up with convulsions and shaken by the vibrations of his growling, seems to piece itself back together again, smoothing itself out and revealing from its depths an almost entirely human countenance. I approach him without fear and undo the buckle on his neck. We now walk side by side. The bookbinder is dressed in respectable black clothing, though he goes barefoot. I try to engage him in conversation, but all that comes out of his mouth is incomprehensible gibberish. Only in his eyes—in those black, expressive eyes—can I read the wild enthusiasm of an affection and sympathy that eases my dread. Occasionally I trip on a stone or a clump of earth; the resulting shock immediately causes his face to crack and disintegrate, his fear half-emerging again, ready to pounce, and right behind it his fury, just waiting for the moment to transform his face back into a nest of hissing vipers. Then I call him to order with a gruff but friendly admonition. I even clap him on the back. Sometimes a surprised, suspicious, incredulous smile tries to form on his face. How burdensome is this dreadful friendship! How terrifying this uncanny affection! How to get rid of this man striding along beside me, his eyes clinging to my face with all the fervour of his doggish soul! Yet I must not betray my impatience. I take out my wallet and say in a matter-of-fact tone: 'You're in need of money, I'm sure. I can lend you some—it would be my pleasure.' But at the sight of the wallet his face takes on a look of such terrifying wildness that I put it away at once. For a long time, he cannot compose himself or control his face, twisted with convulsions of howling. I can't bear it any longer. Anything but this. Matters have already become so hopelessly complicated and entangled. Over the town, I can see the glow of a conflagration. Father is somewhere off amidst the fires of revolution in the burning shop; Doctor Gotard is unreachable; and to top it all off my mother has incomprehensibly appeared incognito on some secret mission! These are the links in the chain of the enormous, unintelligible intrigue slowly tightening around my person. I must escape from here. I must escape. Anywhere. I must throw off this awful friendship with the bookbinder who reeks of dog and who has not taken his eyes off me. We are standing before the entrance to the Sanatorium. 'Please come through to my room,' I say with a polite gesture. Civilized movements fascinate him, soothing his wildness. I usher him into the room in front of me. I sit him down on a chair.

'I'll just go down to the restaurant to fetch some cognac,' I say.

At this, he springs up in terror, eager to accompany me. I calm his panic with gentle firmness.

'You sit here, sir, and wait patiently,' I say in a deep, trembling voice, at the bottom of which a hidden fear can be heard. He sits down with an uncertain smile.

I go out and walk slowly down the corridor, down the stairs, and along the passage to the exit. I step outside, cross the courtyard, slam the iron gate behind me, and begin to run without stopping, heart beating and temples pulsing, along the dark avenue that leads to the train station.

Images pile up in my mind, each more horrific than the last. The impatience of the monster, his terror and despair when he realizes that he has been deceived. The return of his fury, the resurgence of his rage, exploding with irrepressible force. The return of my father to the Sanatorium, his heedless knocking on the door, and the unexpected face-to-face with the terrible beast.

It's just as well that Father is no longer really alive, that the beast cannot reach him, I think with relief, as I see before me a black line of railway cars ready to depart. I get into one of them, and the train moves off slowly without a whistle, as if it had been waiting for me.

Through the window, the vast bowl of the horizon slowly shifts and turns past me once again, swollen with the black, soughing woods, in which the walls of the Sanatorium glow white. Farewell, Father; farewell, town that I will never see again.

Since then, I have been travelling, always travelling. I have somehow made my home on the rails, and they tolerate me here, as I roam from wagon to wagon. The carriages, as enormous as rooms, are filled with rubbish and straw; the draughts drill through them into grey, colourless days.

My clothes are torn and frayed. They have given me a second-hand railwayman's uniform. My face is wrapped in a dirty rag for a swollen cheek. I sit in the straw and doze. When I am hungry, I stand in the corridors between the second-class compartments and sing. They toss small change into my conductor's cap—the black cap of a railwayman, with a ragged peak.

FATHER'S LAST ESCAPE

I T WAS IN the late, careworn period of total disintegration, the period of the final liquidation of our
affairs. The signboard had long since been taken down
from over the door of our shop. Through the half-
lowered shutters, my mother conducted an illicit trade in
the remnants. Adela had left for America. They said her
ship had sunk, and that all the passengers had perished.
We could never verify these rumours, but all news of the
girl ceased and we never heard from her again. A new
era began: empty, sober, joyless, as blank as paper. Our
new servant girl, Genia, floated softly through the
rooms—anaemic, pale, and boneless. When we went to
stroke her on the back, she would writhe about and
stretch herself out like a snake, purring like a cat. She
had milky-white skin; even under the lids of her enam-
elled eyes, she was not pink. Through sheer absentmindedness, she once cooked up a roux from old invoices and
ledgers; it was bland and inedible.

By this time, my father had definitively died. He had died multiple times, but never quite completely, always with certain reservations that necessitated a revision of the fact. This had its bright side. By breaking his death up into instalments, Father was accustoming us to the idea of his departure. We became indifferent to his returns, ever more reduced and pathetic on each occasion. The physiognomy of my now absent father somehow permeated the room in which he had lived, branching out to form bizarre, yet unmistakable nodes of resemblance. In certain places, the wallpaper imitated the convulsions of his nervous twitch, its arabesques forming the painful anatomy of his laugh, broken up into symmetrical limbs like the fossilized prints of a trilobite. For some time, we gave his polecat-lined fur coat a wide berth. The coat breathed. The panic of the little animals—sewn together and biting into one another—ran through it in helpless convulsions that dissipated into the folds of the fur lining. When one put one's ear to it, one could hear the melodic purring of their harmonious slumber. In this well-tanned form, with its slight odour of polecat, slaughter, and nocturnal rutting, he might well have lasted for years. But he did not last long here.

One day, Mother came in from town with a look of dismay on her face. 'Look, Józef,' she said. 'What a piece of work he is! I caught him on the stairs, hopping from step to step.' She lifted a napkin off something she was carrying on a plate. I recognized him at once. The resemblance was unmistakable, though he was now a sort of crayfish or enormous scorpion. We both did a double take, astonished by the distinctness of the resemblance, which despite all the transformations and metamorphoses suggested itself with irresistible force. 'Is he alive?' I asked. 'I tell you, I can barely hold him,' said Mother. 'Should I drop him on the floor?' She laid the plate on the ground. We leant over to inspect him more closely. He was slouched down between long, bowed legs, which he gently moved. His slightly raised pincers and whiskers seemed almost to be listening. I tipped up the plate, and he stepped off it cautiously, somewhat hesitantly, down onto the floor. But as soon as he touched the flat ground beneath him, he took off on his many legs like a shot, his hard arthropod's bones clattering. I blocked his path. He hesitated, feeling the obstacle with his trembling whiskers, then raised his pincers and turned aside. We let him run in his chosen direction. On that side, there was no furniture to give him cover. Running in rippling spasms on his numerous legs, he reached the wall; before we knew it, he had scrambled nimbly up onto it, without stopping, using the whole armature of his limbs. I shuddered with instinctive repulsion as I followed his many-limbed path, rustling over the wallpaper. Soon he reached a little kitchen cupboard built into the wall. For a moment, he flexed his body on its edge, investigating the terrain of the cupboard with his pincers, and then clambered inside.

He became reacquainted with our apartment from this new, crablike perspective, perceiving objects, perhaps by smell, since on closer inspection I could not detect any organ of sight on him. He seemed to ponder for a moment over objects encountered on his path, halting before them, touching them with his rippling whiskers and even embracing them, as if to test them out. He got to know them with his pincers, and only after a moment would he extricate himself and carry on, dragging his abdomen along behind him, slightly raised above the floor. He behaved in the same manner towards the pieces of bread and meat we threw to him on the floor in the hope that he might eat them. He merely pawed at them casually, and then ran on, apparently not perceiving these objects as edible things.

Watching his patient reconnaissance of the room, one could imagine that he was doggedly searching for something. From time to time, he ran into the corner of the kitchen under our leaking water barrel, where he seemed to drink from the puddle. Sometimes he would disappear for days. He seemed to get by perfectly well without food, and we noticed that he did not lose any signs of vigour as a result. With mixed emotions of shame and disgust, we each harboured the secret fear that he might visit us in bed by night. But this did not happen even once, though during the day he clambered all over the furniture, showing a particular fondness for the gap between the cupboards and the wall.

Certain signs of reason, and even a mischievous frivolity, were also unmistakable. For example, Father never failed to appear in the dining room at mealtime, though his participation in the meal was purely platonic. If the door to the dining room happened to be shut and he found himself in the next room, he would rattle away at the bottom of the door, running to and fro along the crack, until someone opened it. Later he learnt to slip his claws and legs through the crack, and after some rather strenuous wriggling managed to squeeze himself sideways under the door into the room. This seemed to please him. Then he froze under the table and lay completely still, with only his abdomen still pulsating. What this rhythmic pulsing of his glossy abdomen meant we could not guess. But it was somehow ironic, indecent, and malicious, seeming to express some base and obscene satisfaction. Nemrod, our dog, approached him slowly and hesitantly, sniffed him with caution, sneezed, and then wandered off indifferently, without having arrived at any definitive judgement.

The disintegration of our home expanded into ever wider circles. Genia slept for days at a time, her slender body rippling bonelessly in time with her deep breathing. In the soup, we would often find sewing pins, which she had thrown in together with the vegetables through inattention and a strange absentmindedness. The shop was open *in continuo*, night and day. The clearance sale took its convoluted course through the half-lowered shutters, day after day, amidst much bargaining and discussion. To cap it all, Uncle Karol arrived.

He was strangely taciturn and disconcerted. He declared with a sigh that in the wake of recent sad experiences he had decided to change his lifestyle and take up the study of languages. He refused to leave the house, locking himself in the spare room, from which Genia had removed all the rugs and wall hangings, filled with disapprobation of our new guest, who promptly immersed himself in the study of old price lists. On several occasions, he attempted to stomp on Father's abdomen. With shouts of terror, we stopped him. He just smiled spitefully to himself, unconvinced, while Father paused attentively over some marks on the floor, unaware of the danger.

My father was swift and agile while still on his feet, but like all crustaceans he became quite defenceless when flipped upside down. It was a sad, pathetic sight, as he spun helplessly on his back around his own axis, his legs waving desperately in the air. One could not look without consternation at the all-too-clear, articulated, almost shameless mechanism of his anatomy, lying on its top, so to speak, unprotected on the side of its bare, multi-sectioned belly. At such moments, Uncle Karol would leap to his feet in a wild attempt to stomp on him. We would rush to the rescue, holding out some object or other, which Father would grip tightly in his pincers to regain his normal position, before immediately taking off in a circuitous run, zigzagging about with redoubled speed, as if he wanted to wipe away the memory of his embarrassing fall.

I must now overcome my reluctance to relate truthfully an incomprehensible event whose reality I still shy away from with my entire being. To this day, I cannot comprehend that we were all its fully conscious perpetrators. In this light, the event almost takes on the aspect of a strange fatalism. For fate does not evade our consciousness or our will, but rather it absorbs them into its mechanism, so that in a daze of lethargy we might permit and accept things from which we would shy away in normal circumstances.

In shock at the accomplished fact, I despairingly asked my mother: 'How could you do this? If at least it was Genia who did it, but you . . .' Mother just wept, wringing her hands, unable to give me an answer. Had she thought things would be better for Father like that? Had she seen it as the only way out of his hopeless situation? Or had she acted from an incomprehensible recklessness or thoughtlessness? . . . Fate may find a thousand tricks by which to impose its incomprehensible will. A temporary lapse of reason or a moment of blindness is all it needs to sneak the deed in between the Scylla and Charybdis of our decisions. Then one can interpret and explain one's motives as much as one likes *ex post*, poring over the reasons, but the accomplished fact remains settled and irreversible, once and for all.

We had come to our senses and shaken off our blindness only when Father was brought in on a platter. He lay there, enormous and swollen from the cooking, pale grey and jellied. We sat there in crestfallen silence. Only Uncle Karol reached out with his fork to the platter, but then hesitantly let it fall halfway, looking at us with astonishment. Mother ordered that the platter be taken into the living room. There it lay on a table covered with a plush cloth, alongside a photo album and a music box filled with cigarettes, motionless and shunned by all of us.

Yet this was not to be the end of my father's earthly wanderings. Indeed, the next instalment—the continuation of the story beyond all permissible limits—is the most painful part. For why did he not give up at long last? Why did he not admit defeat, when he now had every reason to do so, and fate could go no further in its cruel persecution of him? After several weeks lying motionless, he seemed to pull himself together somehow, as if he were slowly recovering. Then one morning we awoke to find the platter empty. Only a single leg lay on the edge of the dish, left behind in the congealed tomato sauce and jelly trampled by his escape. Cooked through, losing legs along the way, he had dragged himself off with the last of his strength into homeless wanderings, and we never laid eyes on him again.

UNDULA

by Marceli Weron [Bruno Schulz]

Bruno Schulz left only two collections of short stories and a few scattered essays behind when he was murdered by a German officer in his home town of Drohobycz in 1942. Since his death, the legend of a great lost work, a novel entitled The Messiah, *has inspired international investigations and even new works by Philip Roth, Cynthia Ozick, and other writers. To this day,* The Messiah *has never been found, and there is no certainty that it ever existed. But an exciting discovery has recently been made in Schulz's native region, today in western Ukraine.*

In 2019, in an archive in Lviv, a Ukrainian researcher named Lesya Khomych found a strange short story in an obscure Polish oil industry newspaper from 1922. Entitled 'Undula', the story follows the masochistic sexual imaginings of a sick man confined to his bed in a room inhabited by whispering shadows and cockroaches. Khomych immediately suspected that Schulz might be the author, though the work appeared under the unknown name of Marceli Weron. Leading experts in Poland soon confirmed her hypothesis.

Though there can be no definitive proof, the story is certainly Schulz's, published under a pseudonym more than a decade before his first known works came out in 1933. The titular 'Undula' is a name Schulz invented for a young woman central to the masochistic sexual mythology of his drawings of the early 1920s. He produced multiple images of an 'Undula' closely fitting the descriptions of the story—a sultry demigoddess spurning the protagonist who worships her. Other distinctive references anticipate characters from Schulz's later stories: a haughty maidservant called Adela, a 'Demiurge' creator, crablike cockroaches, and a sickly protagonist in solitary confinement.

The richly figurative style of the story is also unmistakable, though a slightly uneven quality perhaps reflects its experimental status. Schulz's best writing takes aesthetic risks, as he exuberantly accumulates metaphor upon metaphor. In this early sketch, the result is occasionally awkward or repetitive. Certain meanings remain obscure. Yet the story also contains brilliant passages and stunning new elements that expand our understanding of Schulz.

'Undula' is more frankly sexual than the later stories, which are mostly told from the perspective of a child. Here the adult narrator creates an atmosphere closer to Schulz's erotic drawings, obsessively filled with images of the artist himself grovelling at the feet of lithe young women. The new story almost forms a missing link between the graphical and literary phases of his creative life.

An oil industry newspaper seems a strange place for the original publication of this surrealist work in 1922. The connection here might have been Schulz's elder brother, Izydor, who worked in the oil business that dominated the Drohobycz area. He could have facilitated the publication, with the pseudonym necessitated by his (or Bruno's) embarrassment at the story's candidly sexual content. A decade later, in 1933, Izydor bankrolled his brother's first published volume of stories, Cinnamon Shops *(Sklepy cynamonowe). Perhaps incongruously, it was the oil money of Schulz's native region that underwrote the poetic flights of his literary works.*

The discovery of what is probably Schulz's earliest published story opens the tantalizing possibility that he might have published other works under pseudonyms. Polish and Ukrainian researchers have been combing through archives in both countries for further traces. Eighty years after his murder in the Holocaust, the image of Bruno Schulz's life and work might be far from complete. With the revelation of a new deity in 'Undula', there may yet be hope for those still waiting for The Messiah.

Stanley Bill

* * *

I T MUST BE weeks or months now that I've been locked in this solitude. I keep falling into sleep and then waking again, so that phantoms of wakefulness become tangled with figments of the somnolent darkness. And so time passes. It seems to me that I've lived in this long, crooked room before, in some distant past. Sometimes I recognize the oversized furniture that stretches up to the ceiling, these plain oak wardrobes bristling with dust-covered junk. A large, multi-armed tin lamp hangs from above, swaying gently.

I lie in the corner of a long yellow bed, my body barely filling even a third of its expanse. There are moments in which the room, illumined by the yellow light of the lamp, seems to vanish from my sight. In a heavy lethargy of thought, I feel only the calm, powerful rhythm of my breath, as it raises my chest in a regular beat. In harmony with this rhythm comes the breath of all things.

Time oozes away with the vapid hissing of the oil lamp. The old furniture cracks and creaks in the silence. Shadows lurk and conspire in the depths of the room—jagged, crooked, and broken. They stretch out their long necks and peer at me through their arms. I don't turn over. What for? As soon as I look, they will all be quiet in their places again, and only the floor and the old wardrobe will creak and groan. Everything will be still, unchanged, like before. Once more there will be silence, and the old lamp will sweeten its boredom with a sleepy hiss.

Great, black cockroaches stand motionless, staring vacantly into the light. They seem dead. All of a sudden, those flat, headless bodies take off in an uncanny crab-like run, cutting diagonally across the floor.

I sleep, wake, and then doze off again, patiently pushing my way through sickly thickets of phantoms and dreams. They become tangled and intertwined as they wander along with me—soft, milky, luxuriant bushes, like the pale nocturnal sprouts of potatoes in cellars, like monstrous growths of diseased mushrooms.

*

Perhaps out in the world it's already spring. I don't know how many days and nights have passed since that time ... I remember that grey, heavy dawn of a February day, that purple procession of bacchantes. Through what pale nights of revelry, through what moonlit suburban parks did I not fly after them, like a moth bewitched by Undula's smile. And everywhere I saw her in the shoulders of the dancers: Undula, languid and leaning enticingly in black gauze and pant-ies; Undula, her eyes afire behind the black lace of a fan. And so I followed her with a sweet, burning frenzy in my heart, until my swooning legs would carry me no further and the carnival spat me out, half-dead, on some empty street in the thick gloom before dawn.

Then came those blind wanderings, with sleep in my eyes, up old staircases climbing through many dark stories, crossings of black attic spaces, aerial ascents through galleries swaying in the dark gusts of wind, until I was swallowed up by a quiet, familiar corridor, and found myself at the entrance to our apartment of my childhood years. I turned the handle, and the door opened inward with a dark sigh. The scent of that forgotten interior enfolded me. Our maidservant Adela emerged from the depths of the apartment, padding noiselessly on the velvet soles of her slippers. How she had blossomed in beauty during my absence, how pearly-white her shoulders were under her black, unbuttoned dress. She was not the least bit surprised by my return after all these years. She was sleepy and brusque. I could make out the swan-like curves of her slender legs as she disappeared back into the black depths of the apartment.

I groped my way through the half-light to an unmade bed and, eyes dimming with sleep, plunged my head into the pillows.

Dull sleep rolled over me like a heavy wagon laden with the dust of darkness, covering me with its gloom.

The winter night began to wall itself in with black bricks of nothingness. Infinite expanses condensed into deaf, blind rock: a heavy, impenetrable mass growing into the space between things. The world congealed into nothingness.

*

How difficult it is to breathe in a room caught in the pincers of a winter night. Through the walls and ceiling one can feel the pressure of a thousand atmospheres of darkness. The air is barren, lacking nourishment for the lungs. The light of the lamp is overgrown with black mushrooms. One's pulse becomes faint and shallow. Boredom, boredom, boredom. Somewhere deep in the solid mass of the night, lone wayfarers walk along the dark corridors of the winter. Their hopeless conversations and monotonous tales seem to reach me. Undula reposes in her fragrant bed in a deep slumber that sucks out of her the memory of all the orgies and frenzies. Her limp, soft body—peeled out of the confines of gauze, panties, and stockings—has been snatched up by the darkness, which clutches her in four enormous paws, like a great furry bear, gathering her white, velvety limbs into one sweet handful, over which it pants with purple tongue. And she, unresponsive, her eyes in distant dreams, numbly gives herself over to be devoured, while her pink veins pulsate with milky ways of stars, drunk in by her eyes on those vertiginous carnival nights.

Undula, Undula, o sigh of the soul for the land of the happy and perfect! How my soul expanded in that light, when I stood, a humble Lazarus, at your bright threshold. Through you, in a feverish shiver, I came to know my own misery and ugliness in the light of your perfection. How sweet it was to read from a single glance the sentence condemning me forever, and to obey with the deepest humility the gesture of your hand, spurning me from your banqueting tables. I would have doubted your perfection had you done anything else. Now it is time for me to return to the furnace from which I came, botched and misshapen. I go to atone for the error of the Demiurge who created me.

Undula, Undula! Soon I will forget you too, o bright dream of that other land. The final darkness and the hideousness of the furnace draw near.

*

The lamp filters the boredom, hissing its monotonous song. I seem to have heard it before, long ago, somewhere at the beginning of life, when as a forlorn, sickly infant I fussed and fretted through tearful nights. Who then called out to me and brought me back as I blindly sought the path of return to maternal, primordial nothingness?

How the lamp smokes. The grey arms of the candelabra have sprung out of the ceiling like a polyp. The shadows whisper and plot. Cockroaches scuttle noiselessly across the yellow floor. My bed is so long that I can't see its other end. As always, I am ill, gravely ill. How bitter and filled with abomination is the road to the furnace.

Then it began. These futile, monotonous dialogues with pain have utterly worn me down. Endlessly I argue with it, adamant that it cannot reach me where I exist as pure intellect. While everything else becomes muddled and clouded, I feel ever more clearly how he—the suffering one—is separated from my watching self. And yet at the same time I feel the delicate tickle of dread.

The flame of the lamp burns ever lower and more darkly. The shadows stretch their giraffes' necks up to the ceiling; they want to see him. I hide him carefully away under the quilt. He is like a small, shapeless embryo without face, eyes, or mouth; he was born to suffer. All he knows of life are those forms and monstrosities of suffering that he meets in the depths of the night in which he is plunged. His senses are turned inward, greedily absorbing pain in all its varieties. He has taken my sufferings upon himself. Sometimes it seems he is nothing but a great swim bladder inflated with pain, the hot veins of suffering upon its membranes.

Why do you weep and fuss the whole night through? How can I ease your sufferings, my little son? What am I to do with you? You writhe, sulk, and scowl; you cannot hear or understand human speech; and yet still you fuss and hum your monotonous pain through the night. Now you are like the scroll of an umbilical cord, twisted and pulsating . . .

*

The lamp must have gone out while I dozed. It's dark and quiet now. Nobody weeps. There is no pain. Somewhere deep, deep in the darkness, somewhere beyond the wall, the drainpipes chatter. My God! It is the thaw! . . . The attic spaces dully roar like the bodies of enormous musical instruments. The first crack must have formed in the solid rock of that black winter. Great lumps of darkness loosen and crumble in the walls of the night. Darkness pours like ink through those fissures in the winter, muttering in the drainpipes and sewers. My God, the spring is coming . . .

Out there in the world, the town slowly releases itself from manacles of darkness. The thaw chisels out house after house from that stone wall of darkness. O, to draw in the dark breath of the thaw with my breast again; o, to feel upon my face the black, moist sheets of wind sweeping down the streets. The little flames of the lamps on the street corners shrink into their wicks, turning blue, as those purple sheets of wind flutter around them. O, to steal away now and escape, leaving him alone here forever with his eternal pain . . .

What base temptations do you whisper into my ear, o wind of the thaw? But in what district of the town is that apartment? And where does it face, that window, with its shutter knocking? I cannot remember the name of the street of my childhood home. O, to look out that window and feel the breath of the thaw . . .

STEFAN ZWEIG · EDGAR ALLAN POE · ISAAC BABEL
TOMÁS GONZÁLEZ · ULRICH PLENZDORF · JOSEPH KESSEL
VELIBOR ČOLIĆ · LOUISE DE VILMORIN · MARCEL AYMÉ
ALEXANDER PUSHKIN · MAXIM BILLER · JULIEN GRACQ
BROTHERS GRIMM · HUGO VON HOFMANNSTHAL
GEORGE SAND · PHILIPPE BEAUSSANT · IVÁN REPILA
E.T.A. HOFFMANN · ALEXANDER LERNET-HOLENIA
YASUSHI INOUE · HENRY JAMES · FRIEDRICH TORBERG
ARTHUR SCHNITZLER · ANTOINE DE SAINT-EXUPÉRY
MACHI TAWARA · GAITO GAZDANOV · HERMANN HESSE
LOUIS COUPERUS · JAN JACOB SLAUERHOFF
PAUL MORAND · MARK TWAIN · PAUL FOURNEL
ANTAL SZERB · JONA OBERSKI · MEDARDO FRAILE
HÉCTOR ABAD · PETER HANDKE · ERNST WEISS
PENELOPE DELTA · RAYMOND RADIGUET · PETR KRÁL
ITALO SVEVO · RÉGIS DEBRAY · BRUNO SCHULZ · TEFFI
EGON HOSTOVSKÝ · JOHANNES URZIDIL · JÓZEF WITTLIN